NEW YORK REVIEW BOOKS
CLASSICS

THE SECRET COMMONWEALTH

ROBERT KIRK (1641?–1692) was the seventh son of James Kirk, Minister of Aberfoyle. He studied at Edinburgh and St. Andrews, became Minister of Balquhidder in 1664, and succeeded his father at Aberfoyle in 1685. Kirk published the first Gaelic translation of the Psalms and oversaw the preparation of the first romanized version of the Gaelic Bible. *The Secret Commonwealth* was left in manuscript at the time of his death.

MARINA WARNER's studies of religion, mythology, and fairy tales include *Alone of All Her Sex: The Myth and the Cult of the Virgin Mary*, *From the Beast to the Blonde*, and *Stranger Magic* (National Book Critics Circle Award for Literary Criticism; Truman Capote Award). A Fellow of the British Academy, Warner is also a professor of English and creative writing at Birkbeck, University of London. In 2015 she was given the Holberg Prize and in 2017 she was elected president of the Royal Society of Literature. Her most recent book is *Forms of Enchantment: Writings on Art and Artists*.

THE SECRET COMMONWEALTH

Of Elves, Fauns, and Fairies

ROBERT KIRK

Introduction by
MARINA WARNER

NEW YORK REVIEW BOOKS

New York

THIS IS A NEW YORK REVIEW BOOK
PUBLISHED BY THE NEW YORK REVIEW OF BOOKS
435 Hudson Street, New York, NY 10014
www.nyrb.com

Page 63 shows a detail from Robert Kirk's student notebook; courtesy Edinburgh University Library.

The Library of Congress has cataloged the hardcover edition as follows:
Kirk, Robert, 1641?–1692.
The secret commonwealth: of elves, fauns, and fairies / by Robert Kirk ; introduction by Marina Warner.
p. cm. — (New York Review Books classics)
Originally published: London : D. Nutt, 1893.
ISBN-13: 978-1-59017-177-6 (alk. paper)
ISBN-10: 1-59017-177-2 (alk. paper)
1. Clairvoyance. 2. Fairies. 3. Parapsychology. I. Title.
BF1434.S3K55 2006
130—dc22
2006021076

ISBN 978-1-68137-356-0
Available as an electronic book; ISBN 978-1-68137-357-7

Printed in the United States of America on acid-free paper.
10 9 8 7 6 5 4 3

CONTENTS

INTRODUCTION

"I never could advance my curiosity to conviction; but came away at last only willing to believe."
—Samuel Johnson,
A Journey to the Western Islands of Scotland, 1775

The Times of London recently reported that a property developer in Perthshire, Scotland, had been prevented from breaking the ground for some houses on land he had acquired because there was a fairy stone standing on it. Local people were seriously protesting against its removal.[1] Telephone calls, council meetings, and newspaper interviews confirmed the determination of the objectors: the rock was ancient, it covered the entrance to a fairy fort or hill, and it was extremely unlucky to move any such cromlechs, menhirs, or other ancient monuments because the fairies would be upset . . . and take their revenge. The *Times* reporters joked, dubbing the locals' beliefs "MacFeng shui." They quoted the chairman of the local council with responsibility for granting planning permission: "'I believe in fairies,' she said, 'But I can't be sure they live under that rock.' For her, the rock had historical and sacred importance because it was connected to the Picts and their kings had been crowned there."

The builder's bulldozers were stopped; since then, there has been no more news from St. Fillan's Perthshire.

Perthshire is the county where more than three hundred years ago, the earliest and, to this day, one of the most significant studies of fairyland and fairies was researched and written by a minister of the Scottish Kirk, himself called Robert Kirk. His parish was in Aberfoyle in the Trossachs, about twenty miles from St. Fillan's, surrounded by wild and lonely Highland scenery, and there, in 1691, he compiled the lore and beliefs of his parishioners for an extended essay, *The Secret Commonwealth*, left in manuscript at the time of his death shortly after.[2]

The Reverend Robert Kirk was an Episcopalian minister in the Scottish Highlands, following in his father's footsteps. He was born either in 1641 or 1644, and a seventh son. During his childhood, the family experienced at first hand the violence of the civil war and religious tensions: the Kirks lost their house and all their possessions in the troubles. Questions of the occult and the supernatural were no less close to home, and no less contentious. King James I, formerly King James VI of Scotland, who came to the throne in 1603 on the death of Elizabeth and united the warring kingdoms, was a committed believer in magic powers. In his treatise,

Daemonologie (1597), he had justified his hand in the terrible witch hunts of his time, and throughout Kirk's life, witches continued to be hunted and killed—indeed the last execution was to take place in Scotland as late as 1727, while witchcraft remained a capital offence for another eight years.[3] King James also left his mark in another, profound way long after Cromwell's Commonwealth had come to an end and the Restoration ushered in a new mood: it was his Authorized Version of the Bible, officially distributed throughout the parishes of the realm, that crystallized the newly united nations' consciousness, both with regard to the Protestant faith and the English language.

Robert Kirk was closely touched by these strains in seventeenth-century attitudes: by arguments over heterodox beliefs and religious truth, about national identity, and by the spread of Bible reading. But his ministry, his learning, and his temperament bore him on the current in a different direction from most of his contemporaries: towards a benign and tolerant delight in the breadth of human understanding, imaginings, and possibility. Here was a minister of the Kirk who threw his arms wide to enfold the beliefs of his parishioners, who collected the lore of the people, who was fascinated by their concept of faery. He did not hold with stringent diagnoses of heresy or with rooting it out, but treated popular custom and opinion—and superstition—as worthy of intellectual interest and genuine respect. In *The Secret Commonwealth* and related documents, Kirk set out what he had learned from seers gifted with second sight about the "middle" people, and he wrote down his discoveries without skepticism, let alone scoffing.

The result is a curiosity as well as a book about curiosities, with an affinity to the works of the English antiquarian belle-lettrists of the same era—Sir Thomas Browne, Robert Burton, and John Aubrey. But Kirk's slender opus is far more than a curiosity, or even a miscellany; in *The Secret Commonwealth* he outlines a vigorous, unofficial supernatural system, flourishing as widespread belief in his day. Extant in two manuscripts, this extraordinary treatise was only printed and published for the first time in 1815, more than a hundred years after its composition, through the enthusiasm of Sir Walter Scott[4]; some eighty years after that, Andrew Lang, another prolific and patriotic Scottish writer and collector of local lore, reedited Kirk's text, adding an enthusiastic introduction. In the perspective of the Victorians and the Edwardians, fairies became familiar inhabitants of Romanticism's enchanted realms, and the cult of imagination lifted the suspicion of religious deviancy and popular foolishness that clung to them in Kirk's time.

In any era, however, Kirk's approach to these matters astonishes his readers. For a man of learning to believe in fairy hills, changelings, doppelgängers, and fetches strikes the modern mind as peculiar to say the least; for a man of the cloth to credit men—he was at pains to exclude women[5]—with powers of night-wandering, telepathy, metamorphosis, and healing, appears inconsistent with every religious principle; to believe in such things at all and as seriously as Kirk conveys he does here, can make a reader smile indulgently or even scoff—smug about such fancies in the past.

In the middle to late seventeenth century, there were many among Kirk's contemporaries who also scoffed—empiricists and even atheists who mocked credulity among Christians and heathen likewise; they denounced the persecution of witches and heretics not because they advocated tolerance but because they despised such terrors as reprehensible ignorance and error. The supernatural was a zone of vehement conflict, and the new coffeehouse society in London rang to the arguments of skeptics like Thomas Hobbes, for example, who attributed visions to physiological causes. The new thinking was leading to a denunciation of superstition within established faith; David Hume's critique of miracles was in the making.

To counter the moderns, Thomas Browne protested, "they that doubt of these [Witches] doe not only deny them, but Spirits; and are obliquely and upon consequence a sort, not of Infidels, but of Atheists,"[6] and Christian scholars like Robert Boyle, the eminent chemist, began vigorously mounting a defense of religion through applying empirical methods of inquiry and proof. Browne and Boyle fashioned a scientific hypothesis that telepathy, prophetic dreams, and precognition (second sight) were all forms of consciousness, and that the circumstantial descriptions of fairyland—visible to some, visited by others—offered tangible evidence of other worlds which were congruent with the divine plan of the universe. It was Kirk's particular innovation that in order to give support to claims of uncanny powers, he did not have recourse to the much rehearsed charges against witches, but described with apt, lively detail the parallel realm of "the Subterraneans" as beheld by those who could see them. Fairies became the warranty of preternatural human powers.

Such embattled believers were persuaded that the eternal horizons of Christian cosmology, thronged by individual souls, along with angels and devils, implied a supernatural dimension of experience where hauntings, portents, prophetic dreams, and apparitions were real, not imagined. As the historian Michael Hunter comments, they "sought to vindicate the supernatural by retailing empirical evidence."[7] The Gaelic tradition was fey: the Scots and the Irish entertained traditional uncanny lore about the good folk, the little people, and numbered among them seers "gifted" from birth with second sight, as well as others condemned to the evil eye, so "the Highlands," writes Hunter, "seemed almost like a laboratory, strange yet accessible, where data about abnormal phenomena could be collected and theories tested."[8]

In 1678, Robert Boyle wrote to Lord Tarbat, a Scots nobleman, to inquire into reported powers among the populace; Tarbat responded—in a letter widely circulated in its day—with instances mainly drawn from cases of witchcraft. Fairies, Tarbat reported, seduce "lascivious young men in the quality of succubi or lightsome paramours and strumpets" and they give suck to their familiars. This was the territory of the weird sisters, visited so vividly by Shakespeare in *Macbeth*, and Tarbat's anecdotes capture the darker side of Queen Mab's dream visits and Puck's mischief. Kirk included in *The Secret Commonwealth* a part of Tarbat's letter, which largely corroborated his own ideas about second sight and faery, but he took issue with Tarbat's suspicious tone and disapproval.

Boyle's continued determination to uncover proofs from nature of uncanny lore also inspired him to approach Kirk for information, because, as minister to his remote Highlands parish, Kirk was a Gaelic speaker and scholar. Boyle, who was Anglo-Irish, had commissioned a Bible in Gaelic to help spread the word of the Protestant God in Ireland; asked to distribute this to his exclusively Scots-Gaelic speaking flock, Kirk suggested transliterating the Irish Gaelic into Roman characters, which Boyle agreed to and paid for. "Kirk's Bible," as it came to be known, was published in 1688;

3,000 copies were printed—at the time a vast number for any publication. Kirk also made the first, metrical translation of the Psalms into Gaelic, and he contributed to the catechism in Gaelic—both publications that Boyle underwrote. All this activity overlapped with Kirk's research into fairies and the "gift" of second sight. His later reputation as "Chaplain to the Fairy Queen"—the title Andrew Lang gave him—has rather eclipsed this tribute on his tombstone in Aberfoyle churchyard: *Linguae Hiberniae Lumen,* which translates as "light of the Irish (i.e., Gaelic) tongue."

Kirk went to London under Boyle's patronage and stayed almost a year, supervising the printing of the first Gaelic Bible. While there, he was invited to meet Bishop Edward Stillingfleet and his wife, Elizabeth; the bishop was, like Kirk, a seventh son, and the couple were to bear seven sons. Hearing of Kirk's interests, and knowing the similar circumstances of his birth, they wanted to probe him on the Scottish view of such matters. A passage in Kirk's writings gives us a clue to his personal commitment, when he asks, "why in England the King cures the struma by stroking, and the seventh son in Scotland, whether his temperate complexion conveys a balsam and sucks out the corrupting principles by a frequent warm sanative contact." Kirk never alludes to his own status as a seventh son or to any healing he might have performed, but the accident of his birth must have directed the drift of his interests.

The Stillingfleets had, however, caught the skepticism abroad in the capital, and they expressed doubts about the fairy world, fetches and doubles, apparitions and precognition, stinging their guest into rebuttal. The writing of *The Secret Commonwealth* was the consequence.

After dinner with them, Kirk confided his indignation to his diary:

> It may be supposed not repugnant to Reason or Religion to affect ane invisible polity, or a people to us invisible, having a Commonwealth Laws and Oeconomy, made known to us but by some obscure hints of a few admitted to their converse: because it is no more necessity for us to know there are such Beings and Subterranean Cavern-inhabitants, then it is [necessary] to know distinctly the polity of the 9 orders of Angels, or with what oyl the Lamp of the sun is mainteand, so long and regularly; [or why the moon is called a great Luminary in scripture ...] [or if the moon be inhabited] And if this be thought only a fancy and forgery becaus obscure and unknown to the most of mankind for so long a time, I answer the antipodes and inhabitants of America, the bone of our bone, yet their first discovery was lookt on as a fayrie tale, and the Reporters hooted at as inventers of ridiculous Utopia's. [9]

INTRODUCTION

Running counter to the more traditional model, Kirk's fairy cosmology is not a kingdom ruled by a Fairy King, like Oberon, or a Fairy Queen, whether Titania or Spenser's allegorical figure of English power. Instead, he chooses to characterize it as a commonwealth, and Kirk's fairies are even shown at times to work for the commonweal of human beings. Strikingly, Kirk's vision of the relations between the "subterraneans" and "terrestrials" adopts the language of colonization, and he inverts the historical process of slavery when he imagines that humans all unknowingly toil for the fairies displaced by us from their territory. In a period when planting was the metaphor then used for the settlement of Ireland, Scotland, and points farther afield, including the new empire in the American Indies, Kirk uses the very word "planting" to describe fairies' activity: "We then (the more terrestrial kind), having now so numerously planted all countries, do labour for that abstruse people as well as for ourselves."

Nobody else ever thought of fairyland in this way —not even the utopian dreamers of Victorian and Edwardian children's literature. Again, Kirk does not expand his metaphor, and his unusual usage remains an effect of his personal idiosyncrasy, produced perhaps by his geographical remoteness from the metropolis. The language is nonetheless remarkable, even if we lack grounds to see in it a conscious alignment with radical politics in the aftermath of the Glorious Revolution of 1688 and the reign of William and Mary.

Kirk struck out on his own in other ways as well, fusing two hitherto incommensurate spiritual universes: the fairyland of the Celtic tradition, and the Neo-Platonist world of forms. If his accounts of the fairies echo the language of politics, they also gleam with the transcendence of mystical contemporaries, such as the philosopher Henry More, one of the Cambridge Platonists, who was later to impress his vision powerfully on Coleridge. Kirk describes "the subterranean inhabitants" in material metaphors that recall the language of the poet John Donne: when Kirk describes fairies as "of a middle nature betwixt man and angel" and then restlessly reaches for the right image to evoke their nature ("light, changeable bodies...somewhat of the nature of a condensed cloud," "spongeous, thin, and defaecat," "of congealed air," "chameleon-like bodies [that] swim in the air"), he recalls the twisting wordplay of Donne as he puzzles over the nature of angels in a rapturous sermon of 1627:

> ...that there are distinct orders of *Angels*, assuredly I believe; but what they are, I cannot tell ...They are Creatures, that have not so much of a body as *flesh* is, as *froth* is, as a *vapor* is, as a *sigh* is, and yet with a touch they shall molder a rocke into lesse Atomes, then the sand that it stands

> upon; and a milstone into smaller flower, then it
> grinds... They hang between the nature of God,
> and the nature of man, and are of middle Con-
> dition...[10]

Thinking of fairies as "spirits" and "daemons" in the terms of metaphysical poetry and contemporary Neo-Platonist visions gathers up frequently overlooked and despised popular superstition to a far more respectable sphere; in this, Kirk's eclectic scholarship and his benevolent egalitarianism show a certain daring and agility, whether or not he felt himself to be striking out on a doctrinal limb.[11]

In the steps of his mentor Robert Boyle, Kirk was especially keen to forge an alliance between the latest scientific discoveries, especially in optics, and the preternatural faculties of fairy watchers and walkers, those endowed with second sight, and was by no means alone in accommodating these worlds, so incongruous to our ears now: Robert Hooke, the pioneer of microscopy, had acted as Boyle's technical assistant, and Hooke argued that new optical instruments could restore the perfect faculties which Adam and Eve had enjoyed before the Fall. Kirk might be talking about the past and about ancient superstitions, but he orients his material firmly in the present, and does not reject it, either as falsehood or as heresy. Against Lord Tarbat's condemnation of fairy lore, he argues on two principal counts: first, that such research expands knowledge:

> Therefore every age hath some secret left for its discovery, and who knows but this intercourse betwixt the two kinds of rational inhabitants of the same earth may be not only believed shortly but as freely entertained and as well known as now the art of navigation, printing, gunning, riding on saddles with stirrups, and the discoveries of microscopes which were sometimes as great a wonder and as hard to be believed.

Secondly, Kirk puts the case that fairies not only do not do mischief but offer protection and send "secret intelligence to men." Seers who can receive this intelligence are few, "not of bad lives or addicted to malefices" and so "the true solution of the phenomenon seems rather to be the courteous endeavours of our fellow creatures in the invisible world to convince us...of a deity, of spirits." In this way he shows his unusual "temperate complexion" and applies his characteristic "balsam" to the wounds of religious strife and vehement denunciation that afflicted his century.

The Secret Commonwealth is a work of unusual open-minded syncretism, lively curiosity in people and their ways of being, as well as unusual mild-mannered tolerance. Far from denouncing belief in fairies and stories about them as contrary to Christianity, Kirk considers them compatible, and even welcome; never does he call down the wrath of heaven on his flock or on the seers whose weird experiences he tells. It is not impossible that the permissiveness—and the unorthodoxy—of Kirk's ideas in *The Secret Commonwealth* could have placed him in jeopardy. Whereas several of the strongest believers in Christian dogma were the most ferocious persecutors of witches, and the most uncompromising of Low Church, nonconformist reformers became the most vocal expounders of demons and their menace, Kirk was of an entirely different temper. He remained an Episcopalian, and displays the liberal tendencies of that Church rather than the stringent Puritanism of other Scottish sects.

II

The Secret Commonwealth itself has no precursors; as an account of the fairies and their powers, it is uniquely rich and rare. This "essay of the nature and actions of the subterranean (and for the most part) invisible people, heretofore going under the names of elves, fauns, and fairies, or the like...as they are described by those who have the second sight," now stands as a pioneering piece of ethnographical anthology, whose peculiar interest has sharpened with distance as interest in the uncanny has grown.

When Robert Kirk began gathering fairy lore, one of the theories about the "little people," as they were known, was that they were the remnants of the Picts who had held and ruled Scotland before the coming of the Vikings, the Anglo-Saxons, and others. Defeated and eclipsed, the Picts had, literally, gone underground, and lived in their fairy forts hidden from view of their successors, but audible—on occasion—from the sounds of their hammerings in their tunnels as they worked into tools and jewels the iron and other metals in which they specialized. This view historicized belief in fairies along euhemerist lines, and shaped them in the image of other deposed aboriginal ancestors—making them close cousins of the goldsmithing dwarfs in the Nibelungen sagas. Kirk wrote explicitly to gainsay this line of argument; his book lays out another theory altogether: that fairies exist alongside humans on the one hand, and God and his angels (and the devil and his) on the other, and that they inhabit a parallel universe which disconcertingly impinges and intermingles with men and women.

He glosses the title of his treatise with two subtitles, proclaiming first that it unfolds "the chief curiosities among the people of Scotland," and secondly that they are "for the most part singular to that nation," and that it is a "subject not heretofore discoursed of by any of our writers." So from the opening of his manuscript, the Reverend Kirk gives his document a triple nature—at one level a piece of learned antiquarianism dealing with his nation's *mentalité* and the traditional lore of Gaels, from Ireland and living in Scotland; and at another a collection of linguistic and cultural rarities as if for a connoisseur's cabinet along the lines of Aubrey's *Miscellanies*, as mentioned earlier, and Thomas Browne's inquiries into customs antique and modern. But at a third level, *The Secret Commonwealth* offers an unexpected liberal theology, an unprecedentedly respectful account of popular beliefs and practices. Kirk has some predecessors in the art of encyclopedic eccentricities: the Jesuit Athanasius Kircher; the biologist and doctor Ulisse Aldrovandi in Italy; the mathematician, astrologer, and dream investigator Girolamo Cardano; and, as mentioned earlier, Robert Burton, author of *The Anatomy of Melancholy*. But unlike them, Kirk's work does not make a display of book learning: his pages report mostly what he learned from his parishioners, and resonate with the vigor of the vernacular.

Isolated instances of fairy abductions, apparitions, and changelings appear in the chronicles before Kirk's researches: Geoffrey of Monmouth mentions the boy Elidor, who wandered into fairyland and there stole a golden ball, and Arthurian legends as well as Celtic myths summon up invisible realms and their enchanted inhabitants.[12] Shakespeare's ghosts and dreams—Mercutio's hectic vision of Queen Mab, the pranks of Puck, the "rough magic" of Prospero, and the entranced sleep of many Shakespearean heroines—reveal how Kirk's parishioners' beliefs were not so exclusively Scots or singular or provincial as his local pride lays claim. (Kirk gives no sign of knowing any Shakespeare, and does not compare his findings with similar folklore from poetry and drama such as Robert Herrick's trooping mischief-makers from "Oberon's Feast."[13]) But the end of the seventeenth century saw a new level of curiosity in this European legacy of legends and lore: Kirk is a contemporary of the pioneering writers of fairy tales who, in France, turned away from the classical tradition to find inspiration in vernacular culture: Charles Perrault in *Contes du temps passé* (1697), his younger cousin Marie-Jeanne L'Héritier, and Marie-Catherine d'Aulnoy (*Les Contes de fées*, 1696) all drew on material remembered from their nurses and grandmothers or found in other popular sources.[14]

Kirk combines this now more familiar legacy of poetical fancy with a language—straight, near-scientific —that anticipates that of the anthropologist doing fieldwork, while suffusing the whole of his essay with the rhetorical passion of a minister's sermonizing. He adds no less than six passages from Scripture as his epigraphs, including the shivery lines from Job: "Then a spirit passed before my face, the hair of my flesh stood up..." (Job 4.15–16). His powerful prose sounds cadences and rhythms from the King James Bible, while the juxtaposition of plain vernacular from both English and Scots with esoteric learning intensifies the strangeness of Kirk's diction, and makes his own style exercise a binding fascination on the reader. There is nothing like belief in the reality of something uncanny to summon an atmosphere of queerness. Take Kirk's very first statement (partly quoted earlier) which goes directly to the point:

> These *siths* [pronounced *shee*] or fairies they call ...the good people (it would seem, to prevent the dint of their ill attempts, for the Irish use to bless all they fear harm of) and are said to be of a middle nature betwixt man and angel (as were daemons thought to be of old), of intelligent studious spirits, and light, changeable bodies (like those called astral) somewhat of the nature of a condensed cloud and best seen in twilight.[15]

He goes on to discusses fairies' eating habits, the services they perform for humans—mending shoes and sweeping house and other activities (which led to the naming of the younger branch of the Girl Guides, the "Brownies"); he recounts their form of travel and seasonal migrations. In many ways, their society replicates humans'—they live in houses, marry, give birth, and they even die, his informants reported; and Blake, a hundred years later, would see a fairy funeral. The fairies' social arrangements among themselves as well as their attendance at ours then busies his pen, as Kirk lingers on the weird of doubles—how we might each have a fairy counterpart, a

reflex-man ... or co-walker, every way like the man, as a twin brother and companion, haunting him as his shadow, and is oft seen and known among men (resembling the original) both before and after the original is dead, and was else often seen of old to enter a house, by which these people knew that the person of that likeness was to visit them within a few days. This copy, echo, or living picture goes at last to his own herd. It accompanied that person so long and frequently for ends best known to itself, whether to guard him from the secret assaults of some of its own folks or only as a sportful ape to counterfeit all his actions.

Kirk brings a harsh poetry grounded in the local landscape to the evocation of this phantom figure: the "*heluo* or great-eater" is accompanied by an eerie double, whom he describes as:

a joint-eater or a just-halver, feeding on the pith and quintessence of what the man eats, and that therefore he continues lean like a hawk or heron, notwithstanding his devouring appetite. Yet it would seem they convey that substance elsewhere, for these subterraneans eat but little in their dwellings, their food being exactly clean and served up by pleasant children like enchanted puppets.

Kirk relates more of the fairies' mischief—their stealing and souring milk—in terms similar to the Fairy who interrogates Puck; he tells of fears that they abduct nursing mothers to suckle their own children, leaving behind a phantom baby "like their reflection in a mirror." If you should stumble upon them and reveal their secrets later, they will snatch you under enchantment to live with them. He lists the methods used to ward off such perils—a piece of cold iron in the cot, for fairies abhor this element, which lies near to hell in the underworld, as well as other charms. He discourses learnedly on "elf-bolts" and the harm they do without rupturing the skin. Phrase after phrase in Kirk's short text hangs between metaphor and reality, science and fantasy, learning and lore with irresolvable and often sinister ambiguity: "finding some ease by sojourning and changing habitations, their chameleon-like bodies swim in the air, near the earth with bag and baggage," for example, and then, in another passage, he describes how the fairy women spin "curious cobwebs, impalpable rainbows, and a fantastic imitation of...more terrestrial mortals." How they do this, he adds, "I leave to conjecture."

It is hard sometimes not to feel that he must be smiling.

III

Robert Kirk's ambiguous persuasions—does he really believe all this? how can he?—had an effect on his own afterlife: he became a character like Thomas the Rhymer, the fourteenth-century poet who was stolen away to fairyland when he lay down on a bank, and then returned many years—centuries?—later with the boon—or the bane?—that he could only speak the truth. Like Keats's knight-at-arms "alone and palely loitering," Kirk became himself a victim of the fairies.

Around Aberfoyle, Kirk's last parish, the story began to be told how the minister went out

> walking one evening in his night-gown upon a
> *Dun-shi*, or fairy mount [such as still exists in St.
> Fillan's] in the vicinity of the manse or parsonage, behold! hee sunk down in what seemed to be
> a fit of apoplexy, which the unenlightened took

for death, while the more understanding knew it to be a swoon produced by the supernatural influence of the people whose precincts he had violated.

Walter Scott had the story from Kirk's successor as minister in Aberfoyle[16]; but Scott made it famous by retelling it in his *Letters on Demonology and Witchcraft* (1830). He relates how at the time of Kirk's sudden death, his wife was carrying a baby, destined to be born posthumously, and how after the funeral and burial of the minister in his churchyard, Kirk's ghost appeared to a seer and commanded him to go to a kinsman of Kirk's—Grahame of Duchray. The ghost commanded him, "Say to Duchray, who is my cousin... that I am not dead, but a captive in Fairy Land; and only one chance remains for my liberation." The ghost of Kirk went on to promise that he would make another appearance at his posthumous child's christening: "I will appear in the room, when, if Duchray shall throw over my head the knife or dirk which he holds in his hand, I may be restored to society; but if this opportunity is neglected, I am lost for ever."

So it came about: at the ceremony, the ghost of Robert Kirk appeared while they were seated at table, but his cousin, Grahame of Duchray, was so stunned by the vision that he failed to move quickly enough and throw the cold iron to ward off Kirk's invisible fairy captors. And so "it is to be feared that Mr Kirke still 'drees his weird in Fairy Land.'"

Kirk's grave in the churchyard was empty, Scott was told: "The Light of the Irish Tongue" had melted into the body of many Tannhauser figures of myth and legend, and become a character in the eerie tales he told. Scott sees this as a "terrible visitation of fairy vengeance."[17]

At the same time as this legend began circulating, against a background of the violent conflicts between England and Scotland that erupted again in the mid-eighteenth century, James Hogg published *The Private Memoirs and Confessions of a Justified Sinner* (1824), the greatest achievement of Northern Gothic. *The Private Memoirs* dramatized the tension between hallucination and supernatural truth, between diabolical possession and mental derangement in terms that Kirk does not attempt; nevertheless, Kirk's charting the subterranean regions of Scottish fantasy had opened a different topography of possible enchantment for writers to explore.

Hogg began life as a farmhand who taught himself to read from his employer's library, and came to Edinburgh to write; dubbed "the Ettrick Shepherd," he became Scott's closest protégé, and a friend and collaborator on the project of a national consciousness. The uncanny was central to this enterprise, and remains a singularly potent element in Scotland's culture, much stimulated by the Romantics' interest in local traditions, stories, and ballads.

It is easy to see this concern as a reaction to the ascendancy of Scottish enlightened rationalism, in counterpoint to the deliberate and sober philosophy of Hume, the passionate humane advocacy of the abolitionists and the reformers, and the down-to-earth sense of Dr. Johnson. But interpreting the love of the irrational along these familiar lines (a version of the return of the repressed) misses a deeper and more fruitful connection between reason and the supernatural that led even Dr. Johnson to investigate reported wonders. Here again Kirk's openness offers a clue that points the way. In his essay, the mysteries and horrors of the occult represent a test case for understanding and its ideal Enlightenment counterparts, liberty and tolerance. The uncanny does not call for dismissal; rather it summons into play what Jorge Luis Borges later called "reasoned imagination." Inquiring into folklore, penetrating to the depths of beliefs, fears, and even madness redrafted the contours of experience and consciousness in such a way as to require some kind of intelligent, sympathetic, reflective response—which is not the same as gullibility or complaisance.

By the end of the nineteenth century, however, when the Scottish folklorist, fairy-tale collector, and writer Andrew Lang produced his edition of Kirk's essay, the spellbound fate of "the Fairy Minister," as he also called Kirk, had become an intrinsic and whimsical element of the reception of *The Secret Common-*

wealth and its author. Kirk's explorings had become a folksy relic, suffused with nostalgia for an era where such beliefs were held. Kirk himself had come to seem quixotic, a man caught in a quaint and singular creed. When Lang edited *The Secret Commonwealth* for his handsome edition in 1893, he dedicated it to Robert Louis Stevenson, the most accomplished teller of uncanny tales in the Scottish tradition of faery, who pays homage to Hogg in his famous tale of hauntings and doubles, *The Strange Case of Dr. Jekyll and Mr. Hyde.* Lang connected himself to these national adepts of the uncanny, adding a valedictory poem that pictures Stevenson sadly exiled in his tomb far from the land of kelpies, banshees, and ghasts; it closes with a prayer:

Faith, they might steal *me*, wi' ma will,
And, ken'd I ony Fairy hill,
I'd lay me down there, snod and still,
   Their land to win,
For, man, I've moistly had my fill
   O' this world's din.[18]

Lang thus places himself in an enchanted lineage that runs back via Stevenson to Kirk, and, by this date, envies the Fairy Minister his legendary fate.[19]

And yet even at this rather belated moment, the originality of Kirk's voice still makes itself felt. Lang's lengthy introduction ranges over many topics, coming at the end to a subject close to his heart: psychic research. He compares the seers of the fairies with telepathic mediums of the Victorian era, when Spiritualism and Theosophy were growing in strength of numbers and respectability. W. B. Yeats, Lang's contemporary, was even more deeply immersed in the occult at the time, relying on channelers and automatists to revive his inspiration; while Lang was working to rekindle the legacy of Celtic legend and fairy in Scotland, Yeats wrote to regain the lost time of Celtic fairies, and alongside his friends Speranza Wilde (Oscar's mother) and Lady Gregory, his aesthetic and political ally and associate, he became the catalyst of the return to fairyland. They all collected in the spirit of Kirk, with an equal desire to uncover what he had called "the singularity of the nation." Yeats made common cause over belief in the fairies between the Scots and the Irish against the English, denouncing the latter for dullness of wit and fancy, and declaring that "the world is ... more full of significance to the Irish peasant than to the English. The fairy populace of hill and lake and woodland have helped to keep it so."[20] For Yeats, fairyland ensured poetry. He quotes a Gaelic proverb as an example of the vitality of mind and language that he prized and that was connected to fairy lore: "The lake is not burdened by its swan, the steed by its bridle, or a man by the soul that is in him."[21]

———

Few believe in fairies, now or ever; many have believed that others believe in them, and at different times have engaged passionately by proxy in the phenomenon. Most of the accounts that have survived report incidents and adventures that occurred to someone else. This is the terrain of anecdote and old wives' tales, of oral tradition, hearsay, superstition, and the shaggy dog story: once upon a time and far away among another people ... The greatest writers about fairylands —from Shakespeare to Christina Rossetti to Yeats— summon up Queen Mab, Oberon, and Robin Goodfellow or Puck in all their peculiar detail and woo their audiences to surrender to these "antique fables and fairy toys," but they bend the material through dream frames that distance it from immediate experience. Like medieval kings who kept a ragged and filthy hermit at court to pray on their behalf, we—skeptical, worldly dwellers in culture's mindscapes—need others to stand in for us, changelings of a different sort, to prevent the deforestation and depopulating of fancy's traditional territory. J. M. Barrie dramatized this maneuver of belief by proxy in the play of *Peter Pan*, in the famous scene when the fairy Tinkerbell drinks poison and Peter turns to the audience and tells them to clap their hands to save her.[22] This emotional blackmail—with its shameless pulling of heartstrings—remains fractured by the irony that however loud we clap to show our faith, Barrie isn't sincere, and neither are we, and if the children are with us, they are our dupes.[23]

In the twenty-first century, inquiry into consciousness and altered states has intensified in the sciences on the one hand, while, on the other, fascination with belief, illusion, and subjectivity's inconsistencies increasingly characterizes the concerns of writers and artists. (To give just two examples, the Cottingley Fairy photographs, taken by two young girls in the 1920s and notoriously authenticated by Sir Arthur Conan Doyle, have inspired at least two novels and films, as well as several contemporary artworks, while Julian Barnes's 2005 novel, *Arthur & George*, explores the many paradoxes in Conan Doyle's character.) When Gilles Deleuze and Félix Guattari called, a decade or more ago, for the re-enchantment of the universe, they were defying by implication the contempt for mythmaking, magic, and superstition that both Enlightenment thinkers and later interrogators of the Enlightenment such as Adorno had expressed in scorching terms: "Occultism is the metaphysic of dunces," wrote Adorno, among other remarks of this nature. Enchantment had not been invoked with positive meaning in intellectual or political circles for a long time; it had become the ambition of commercial entertainment—"some enchanted evening" is a typical debased Hollywood anthem. The concept of enchantment trailed, and still does trail, a whiff of deception, illusion, brainwashing —opiates of the imagination. Like other magic words, especially adjectives, that have lost caste—"glamorous," "wicked," as well as "enthralling," and "magical"—this concept of bastard fraudulence now offers a zone of interest, open for re-exploration. States of enchantment, whether wrought by fairies in seventeenth-century Scotland, or attributed to occult or paranormal powers by Victorian psychic researchers, present ways of analyzing consciousness and the self which can illuminate contemporary psychological concerns (for example, cultic possession; recovered memory; alien abduction); numerous contemporary novelists, from Stephen King to Margaret Atwood reflect the revival of this occult approach to personal complexity.[24]

But what connects Robert Kirk's essay to us today is his spirit of active wonder, at once proto-scientific and more than scientific. He is also engagingly singular—a different voice and a fascinatingly unusual companion, confiding in us across the centuries. There is a sense of an enigma tugging at him personally and with some urgency: "Why," Kirk asks, "is not the seventh son infected himself by that contagion he extracts from another?" Puzzling over his inheritance and the beliefs and experiences of his neighbors and his flock, he gave his puzzlement literary expression of a rare order; his capacity to question wonderingly turned him into a remarkable investigator, whom people trusted; it made him, during a lifetime when religious dissension continued to scar society, a proponent of curiosity as a form of tolerance; it also turned him into the most absorbing interpreter of fairy lore, with a true story-teller's gift of communicating a fantastic other world.

—MARINA WARNER

NOTES

I would like to thank Bob Davis, at the University of Glasgow, for his many helpful thoughts and references.

1. Will Pavia and Chris Windle, "Fairies stop developers' bulldozers in their tracks," *The Times* (London), November 21, 2005, p. 5.

2. Louis Stott, "Robert Kirk," *Dictionary of National Biography*, http://www.oxforddnb.com/view/article/15651.

3. See Christina Larner, *Enemies of God: The Witch-hunt in Scotland* (Johns Hopkins University Press, 1981).

4. Sir Walter Scott claimed to have seen an edition of the book published in 1691, but no such edition has ever been traced; it is now thought that he must have made a mistake and been referring to the manuscript.

5. It strikes me that Kirk might have insisted on women's absence from the ranks of seers in order to avoid identifying the practices he is describing with witchcraft—though there

were a few men accused of witchcraft in Scotland as well as women.

6. Thomas Browne, "Religio Medici," in *Thomas Browne: The Major Works,* ed. C. A. Patrides (Harmonsworth: Penguin, 1977), p. 98.

7. Michael Hunter, introduction to *The Occult Laboratory: Magic, Science and Second Sight in Late 17th-Century Scotland,* Michael Hunter, ed. (Bury St. Edmunds: The Boydell Press, 2001), p. 1.

8. Hunter, p. 1.

9. Robert Kirk, *London Journal,* quoted in *The Secret Commonwealth & A Short Treatise of Charms and Spells,* Stewart Sanderson, ed. (London: The Folklore Society, 1976), p. 15. Sanderson suggests that Kirk addressed *The Secret Commonwealth* to Elizabeth Stillingfleet after this visit.

10. John Donne, "A Sermon Preached at the Earl of Bridgewater's house in London at the marriage of his daughter, the Lady Mary, to the Eldest son of the Lord Herbert of Castle-iland, November 19, 1627," in *The Sermons of John Donne*, ed. Evelyn M. Simpson and George R. Potter, 10 vols. (University of California Press, 1956), vol. 8, pp. 94–109.

11. See Mario M. Rossi (d. 1971 Edinburgh), *Il Regno segreto* (reprint, Milan: Adelphi Edizione, 1980; originally *Il capellano delle fate* [Naples: Giannini, 1964]) for a learned exploration of Kirk's reading and connections with philosophy in his time.

12. See W. B. Yeats, *The Celtic Twilight* (1893; reprint, Gerrards Cross, 1981); Thomas Keightley, "The Scottish Highlands," in *The Fairy Mythology: Illustrative of the Romance and Superstition of Various Countries* (London: George Bell and Sons, 1905), pp. 385–396; Katharine Briggs, *The Fairies in*

INTRODUCTION

Tradition and Literature (London: Routledge and Kegan Paul, 1967; reprint, 2002); Briggs, "Some Late Accounts of the Fairies," *Folklore* 72 (September 1961), pp. 509–519; Laurence Harf-Lancner, *Les Fées au moyen-âge: Morgane et Mélusine La Naissance des fées* (Geneva: Editions Slatkine, 1984); Marina Warner, *From the Beast to the Blonde: On Fairytales and Their Tellers* (London: Chatto & Windus, 1994), pp. 3–11. See also Marie Heaney, *Over Nine Waves: A Book of Irish Legends* (Faber and Faber, 1994), and Ciaran Carson, *Fishing for Amber: A Long Story* (London: Granta, 1999) for two powerfully imaginative contemporary retellings.

13. From *Hesperides*, in *The Poetical Works of Robert Herrick*, F. W. Moorman, ed. (Oxford: Clarendon Press, 1915), pp. 119–120, 165–169.

14. Madame d'Aulnoy is credited with printing the first example of the modern literary fairy tale, "L'Ile de la Félicité," which is set in a parallel fairyland, and was interpolated into her novel *L'Histoire d'Hypolite, Comte de Duglas* (a Scottish allusion) in 1690; L'Héritier's first collection, *Oeuvres Meslées*, appeared in 1695; the most influential collection of all was Perrault's *Contes du temps passé*, in 1697, but he began publishing tales in 1694.

15. This twilight is likely to be morning, not evening, the passage from night to day at dawn, not sunset, when dewy mists lie on fields. Yeats, in his essays in *The Celtic Twilight*, reveals this now unfamiliar but crucial metaphor-ical meaning. Thus: "The grey of the morning is the Irish witches' hour..." from "Tales of the Twilight," a review of Lady [Speranza] Wilde, *Ancient Cures, Charms, and Usages of Ireland*, the *Scots Observer, March 1, 1890*, in *Uncollected Prose by W. B. Yeats*, vol. 1, *First Reviews and Articles,*

1886–1896, John P. Frayne, ed. (London: Macmillan, 1970), pp. 169-173.

16. Patrick Grahame, *Sketches of Perthshire* (Edinburgh: Peter Hill, 1812).

17. Walter Scott, *Letters on Demonology and Witchcraft* (London: John Murray, 1830), pp. 163–166; the legend has been revisited by Robert Crawford in a poem, "After Gaelic," which he kindly let me see in 2004.

18. Andrew Lang, ed., *The Secret Commonwealth of Elves, Fauns & Fairies: A Study in Folk-Lore & Psychical Research* (London: David Nutt, 1893; scanned at sacred-texts.com, February 2004, John Bruno Hare, redactor), p.vi.

19. See Lang, p.7:

> And half I envy him who now,
>> Clothed in her Court's enchanted green,
> By moonlit loch or mountain's brow
>> Is Chaplain to the Fairy Queen.

20. See "Irish Fairies, Ghosts, and Witches, etc.," "Fairy Doctors," "The Sociable Fairies," "The Solitary Fairies," "Tales from the Twilight," "Irish Fairies" in *Uncollected Prose by W. B. Yeats*, vol. 1. I am indebted to Roy Foster for bringing these pieces to my attention. See also W. B. Yeats, *Fairy and Folk Tales of the Irish Peasantry* (London: Walter Scott, 1888) and *The Celtic Twilight*.

21. Yeats, "Irish Fairies," Frayne, p. 182; compare "A Remonstrance with Scotsmen for having soured the disposition of their ghosts and faeries," which decides "different ways of looking at things have influenced in each country the whole world of sprites and goblins. For their gay and graceful doings you must go to Ireland; for their deeds of terror to Scotland," in Yeats, *The Celtic Twilight*, pp. 124–126.

22. Barrie on fairies: "they are nearly all dead now... When the first baby laughed for the first time, the laugh broke into a thousand pieces and they all went skipping about, and that was the beginning of fairies. And now when every new baby is born its first laugh becomes a fairy... Children know such a lot now. Soon they don't believe in fairies, and every time a child says, 'I don't believe in fairies' there is a fairy somewhere that falls down dead." J. M. Barrie, *Peter Pan; or, The Boy Who Would Not Grow Up* in *The Plays of J.M. Barrie* (London: Hodder and Stoughton, 1928), p. 32.

23. See Jacqueline Rose, *The Case of Peter Pan; or, the Impossibility of Children's Fiction* (London: Macmillan, 1984). In one of the last stories he wrote, "Farewell Miss Julie Logan" (1932), Barrie's haunted protagonist is a minister newly arrived in the manse in a remote valley; his visitor—a seductive young woman—turns out to be a Catholic from the former time, and he drowns her in the burn rather than succumb to her fatal charms. There are echoes of Kirk's life and legend here, and Barrie seems to be allegorizing Kirk's interest in the fairies as temptation to stray to the "old Religion." See J. M. Barrie, *Farewell Miss Julie Logan: A Barrie Omnibus*, Andrew Nash, ed. (Edinburgh: Canongate, 2000).

24. I have explored this argument more fully in *Phantasmagoria: Spirit Visions, Metaphors, and Media* (Oxford University Press, 2006).

THE SECRET COMMONWEALTH

OR

A TREATISE DISPLAYING THE CHIEF CURIOSITIES AMONG THE PEOPLE OF SCOTLAND AS THEY ARE IN USE TO THIS DAY

Being for the most part singular
to that nation

A subject not heretofore discoursed of
by any of our writers

Done for the satisfaction of his friends
by a modest inquirer, living among
the Scottish-Irish

This edition of *The Secret Commonwealth* observes modern conventions of spelling and punctuation, introduces a number of paragraph breaks, and silently corrects a handful of what have been deemed slips of the scribal pen. Archaic words are spelled in accordance with the *Oxford English Dictionary*. Celtic words, transcribed irregularly in the two slightly different manuscripts of Kirk's essay, have been glossed insofar as possible. There has been no effort to update Celtic orthography, or to correct the garbled Latin, Greek, and Aramaic in the spells that Kirk reproduces. Kirk's essay is now widely known by the title that Andrew Lang gave it in 1893, which we have retained. In establishing the text and in preparing the notes we have consulted the careful transcriptions of Kirk's manuscript made available by Stewart Sanderson in 1976 for the Folklore Society, London, and in Michael Hunter's study of seventeenth-century science, *The Occult Laboratory*, the assistance of which we gratefully acknowledge. All errors are of course our own.

This is a rebellious people, which say to the seers see not; and to the prophets, prophesy not unto us right things but smooth things.

—ISAIAH 30.9–10

And the man, whose eyes were open, hath said . . .

—NUMBERS 24.15

For now we see through a glass, darkly, but then face to face . . .

—I CORINTHIANS 13.12

It doth not yet appear what we shall be; but we shall be like God, and see him as he is.

—I JOHN 3.2

Shall the dead be borne under the waters, and the inhabitants thereof?

—JOB 26.5

Then a spirit passed before my face, the hair of my flesh stood up. It stood still, but I could not discern the form thereof: an image was before my eyes.

— JOB 4.15–16

AN ESSAY

Of the nature and actions of the subterranean (and for the most part) invisible people, heretofore going under the names of elves, fauns, and fairies, or the like, among the low-country Scots, and termed hubhrísgedh, caiben, lusbartan, *and* siotbrudh *among the tramontanes or Scottish-Irish, as they are described by those who have the second sight, and now, to occasion further enquiry, collected and compared.*

With an account of the Irish charms—being part of a larger discourse, of the ancient customs of the Scottish-Irish, their nature, habit, manner of war, husbandry, the air and productions of their country, etc.

I.

OF THE SUBTERRANEAN INHABITANTS

1. These *siths* or fairies they call *sluagh maithe* or the good people (it would seem, to prevent the dint of their ill attempts, for the Irish use to bless all they fear harm of) and are said to be of a middle nature betwixt man and angel (as were daemons thought to be of old), of intelligent studious spirits, and light, changeable

bodies (like those called astral) somewhat of the nature of a condensed cloud and best seen in twilight. These bodies be so pliable through the subtlety of the spirits that agitate them that they can make them appear or disappear at pleasure. Some have bodies or vehicles so spongeous, thin, and defaecat that they are fed by only sucking into some fine spirituous liquor that pierces like pure air and oil; others feed more gross on the foison or substance of corns and liquors or on corn itself that grows on the surface of the earth, which these fairies steal away, partly invisible, partly preying on the grain as do crows and mice. Wherefore in this same age they are sometimes heard to bake bread, strike hammers, and to do suchlike services within the little hillocks where they most haunt, some whereof of old, before the Gospel dispelled paganism, and in some barbarous places as yet, enter houses after all are at rest and set the kitchens in order, cleansing all the vessels. Such drudges go under the name of brownies. When we have plenty, they have scarcity at their homes, and on the contrary (for they are not empowered to catch as much prey everywhere as they please). Their robberies notwithstanding, they oftimes occasion great ricks of corn not to bleed so well (as they call it) or prove so copious by very far as was expected by the owner.

Their bodies of congealed air are sometimes carried aloft, otherwhiles grovel in different shapes, and enter in any cranny or cleft of the earth (where air enters) to their ordinary dwellings, the earth being full of cavities and cells and there being no place or creature but is supposed to have other animals (greater or lesser) living in or upon it as inhabitants and no such thing as a pure wilderness in the whole universe.

2. We then (the more terrestrial kind), having now so numerously planted all countries, do labour for that abstruse people as well as for ourselves. Albeit when several countries were uninhabited by us, these had their easy tillage above ground as we now, the print of whose furrows do yet remain to be seen on the shoulders of very high hills, which was done when the champaign ground was wood and forest.

They remove to other lodgings at the beginning of each quarter of the year, so traversing till doomsday, being impatient of staying in one place and finding some ease by sojourning and changing habitations. Their chameleon-like bodies swim in the air; near the earth with bag and baggage. And at such revolution of time, seers or men of the second sight (females being but seldom so qualified) have very terrifying encounters with them, even on highways; who therefore usually shun to travel abroad at these four seasons of the year and thereby have made it a custom to this day among the Scottish-Irish to keep church duly every first Sunday of the quarter, to sain or hallow themselves, their corns, and cattle from the shots and stealth of these wandering tribes. And many of these superstitious people will not been seen in church again till the next quarter begin, as if no duty were to be learned or done by them, but all the use of worship and sermons were to save them from those arrows that fly in the dark.

They are distributed in tribes and orders and have children, nurses, marriages, deaths, and burials in appearance even as we (unless they so for a mock-show or to prognosticate some such thing to be among us).

3. They are clearly seen by these men of the second sight to eat at funeral banquets. Hence many of the Scottish-Irish will not taste meat at those meetings, lest they have communion with or be poisoned by them. So are they seen to carry the bier or coffin with the corpse, among the middle-earth men, to the grave. Some men of that exalted sight (whether by art or nature) have told me they have seen at those meetings a double-man, or the shape of the same man in two places (that is, a superterranean and subterranean inhabitant perfectly resembling one another in all points), whom he notwithstanding could easily distinguish one from another by some secret tokens and operations, and so go speak to the man his neighbour and familiar, passing by the apparition or resemblance of him.

They avouch that every element and different state of being have animals resembling those of another element, as there be fishes sometimes caught at sea resembling monks of late order in all their hoods and dresses, so as the Roman invention of good and bad daemons and guardian angels particularly assigned is called by them an ignorant mistake sprung only from this original. They call this reflex-man a *coimimechd* or co-walker, every way like the man, as a twin brother and companion, haunting him as his shadow, and is oft seen and known among men (resembling the original) both before and after the original is dead, and was else often seen of old to enter a house, by which these people knew that the person of that likeness was to visit them within a few days. This copy, echo, or living picture goes at last to his own herd. It accompanied that person so long and frequently for ends best known to itself, whether to guard him from the secret assaults of some of its own folks or only as a sportful ape to counterfeit all his actions. However the stories of old witches prove beyond contradiction that all sorts of spirits which assume light airy bodies, or crazed bodies coacted by foreign spirits, seem to have some pleasure (at least to assuage some pain or melancholy) by frisking and capering like satyrs, or whistling and shrieking like unlucky birds, in their unhallowed synagogues and sabbaths. If invited and earnestly required, these companions make themselves known and familiar to men. Otherwise, being in a different state and element, they neither can nor will easily converse with them.

They avouch that a *heluo* or great-eater hath a voracious elf to be his attender called *ceart-coimithech*, a joint-eater or a just-halver, feeding on the pith and quintessence of what the man eats, and that therefore he continues lean like a hawk or heron, notwithstanding his devouring appetite. Yet it would seem they convey that substance elsewhere, for these subterraneans eat but little in their dwellings, their food being exactly clean and served up by pleasant children like enchanted puppets. What food they extract from us is conveyed to their homes by secret paths (as some skilful women do the pith of milk from their neighbours' cows into their own cheese-hold through a hair-tether), at a great distance by art, magic, or by drawing a spigot fastened in a post, which will bring milk as far off as a bull will be heard to roar. The cheese made of the remaining milk of a cow thus strained will swim in water like cork. The method they take to recover their milk is a bitter chiding of the suspected enchanters, charging them by a counter-charm to give them back their own in God or their master's name. But a little of the mother's dung stroked on the calf's mouth before it suck any does prevent this theft.

4. Their houses are called large and fair and (unless at some odd occasions) unperceivable by vulgar eyes, like Rachland and other enchanted islands, having for light continual lamps and fires, often seen without fuel to sustain them. Women are yet alive who tell they were

taken away when in child-bed to nurse fairy children, a lingering voracious image of theirs being left in their place (like their reflection in a mirror), which (as if it were some insatiable spirit in an assumed body) made first semblance to devour the meat that it cunningly carried by and then left the carcass as if it expired and departed thence by a natural and common death. The child and fire, with food and all other necessaries, are set before the nurse, how soon she enters, but she neither perceives any passage out nor sees what these people do in other rooms of the lodging. When the child is weaned or dies, the nurse is conveyed back or gets it to her choice to stay there. But if any superterranean be so subtle as to practice sleights for procuring a privacy to any of their mysteries (such as making use of their ointments, which, as Gyges's ring, makes them invisible or nimble, or cast them in a trance, or alters their shape, or makes things appear at a vast distance, etc.), they smite them without pain, as with a puff of wind, and bereave them of both the natural and acquired sights in the twinkling of an eye (both these sights where once they come being in the same organ and inseparable) or they strike them dumb. The tramontanes to this day put bread, the Bible, or a piece of iron in women's bed when travailing to save them from being thus stolen. And they commonly report that all uncouth unknown wights are terrified by nothing earthly so much as by cold iron. They deliver the reason to be that Hell lying betwixt the chill tempests and the firebrands of scalding metals and iron of the north (hence the lodestone causes a tendency to that point), by an antipathy thereto, these odious far-senting creatures shrug and fright at all that comes thence, relating to so abhorred a place, whence their torment is either begun or feared to come hereafter.

5. Their apparel and speech is like that of the people and country under which they live: so are they seen to wear plaids and variegated garments in the Highlands of Scotland and *suanochs* heretofore in Ireland. They speak but little and that by way of whistling—clear, not rough. The very devils conjured in any country do answer in the language of the place, yet sometimes these subterraneans speak more distinctly than at other times. Their women are said to spin very fine, to dye, to tissue and embroider, but whether it be as manual operation of substantial refined stuffs with apt and solid instruments, or only curious cobwebs, impalpable rainbows, and a fantastic imitation of the actions of more terrestrial mortals, since it transcended all the senses of the seer to discern whether, I leave to conjecture as I found it.

6. Their men travel much abroad, either presaging or aping the dismal and tragical actions of some amongst us, and have also many disastrous doings of their own,

as convocations, fightings, gashes, wounds, and burials, both in the earth and air. They live much longer than we yet die at last, or least vanish from that state. For 'tis one of their tenets that nothing perisheth, but (as the Sun and year) everything goes in a circle, lesser or greater, and is renewed and refreshed in its revolutions, as 'tis another that every body in the creation moves (which is a sort of life), and that nothing moves but has another animal moving on it, and so on, to the utmost minutest corpuscle that's capable to be a receptacle of life.

7. They are said to have aristocratical rulers and laws, but no discernible religion, love, or devotion towards God, the Blessed Maker of All. They disappear whenever they hear His name invoked or the name of Jesus (at which all do bow willingly or by constraint that dwell above or beneath within the earth [Philippians 2.10]), nor can they act aught at that time after hearing of that sacred name. The *tabhaisder* or seer that corresponds with this kind of familiars can bring them with a spell to appear to himself or others when he pleases as readily as Endor Witch did those of her own kind. He tells they are ever readiest to go on hurtful errands, but seldom will be the messengers of a great good to men. He is not terrified with their sight when he calls them, but seeing them in a surprise (as often he does) frights him extremely. And glad he would be quit of

such, for the hideous spectacles seen among them, as the torturing of some wight, earnest ghastly staring looks, skirmishes, and the like. They do not all the harm which appearingly they have power to do, nor are they perceived to be in great pain, save that they are usually silent and sullen. They are said to have many pleasant toyish books, but the operation of these pieces only appears in some paroxysms of antic corybantic jollity—as if ravished and prompted by a new spirit entering into them at that instant, lighter and merrier than their own. Other books they have of involved abstruse sense, much like the Rosicrucian style. They have nothing of the Bible save collected parcels for charms and counter-charms, not to defend themselves withal but to operate on other animals, for they are a people invulnerable to our weapons. And albeit werewolves' and witches' true bodies are (by the union of the spirit of nature that runs through all, echoing and doubling the blow towards another) wounded at home when the astral assumed bodies are stricken elsewhere (as the strings of a second harp tuned to a unison sound though only one be struck), yet these people have not a second or so gross a body at all to be so pierced, but as air, which when divided unites again. Or if they feel pain by a blow, they are better physicians than we and quickly cure it. They are not subject to sore sicknesses, but dwindle and decay at a certain period, all about one age.

Some say their continual sadness is because of their pendulous state (like those men in Luke 13.26), as uncertain what at the last revolution will become of them when they are locked up into an unchangeable condition. And if they have any frolic fits of mirth, 'tis as the constrained grinning of a mort-head, or rather as acted on a stage and moved by another, than cordially coming of themselves.

But other men of the second sight, being illiterate and unwary in their observations, vary from these, one averring those subterranean people to be departed souls attending awhile in this inferior state and clothed with bodies procured through their alms-deeds in this life (called *cuirp dhaondachbach*, viz. fluid, active, ethereal vehicles) to hold them, that they may not scatter, nor wander and be lost in the *totum* or their first nothing. But if any were so impious as to have given no alms, they say when the souls of such do depart, they sleep in an unactive state till they resume the terrestrial bodies again. Others, that what the low-country Scot calls a wraith, and the Irish *éug* or death's messenger (appearing sometimes as a little rough dog, and if crossed and conjured in time will be pacified by the death of any other creature instead of the sick man), is only exuvious fumes of the man approaching death, exhaled and congealed into a various likeness (as ships and armies are sometimes shaped in the air), and called astral bodies, agitated as wildfire with wind, and are neither souls nor counterfeiting spirits. Yet not a few avouch (as is said) that surely these are a numerous people by themselves, having their own polities. Which diversity of judgments may occasion several inconsonancies in this rehearsal, after the narrowest scrutiny made about it.

8. Their weapons are mostwhat solid earthy bodies, nothing of iron but much of a stone, like to yellow soft flint shaped like a barbed arrowhead, but flung as a dart with great force. These arms (cut by art and tools it seems beyond human) have somewhat of the nature of thunderbolt, subtly and mortally wounding the vital parts without breaking the skin, of which wounds, some I have observed in beasts and felt them with my hands. They are not as infallible Benjamites, hitting at a hairsbreadth, nor are they wholly unvanquishable, at least in appearance.

The men of that second sight do not discover strange things when asked, but at fits and raptures, as if inspired with some genius at that instant, which before did lurk in or about them. Thus I have frequently spoke to one of them, who in his transport told he cut the bodies of one of these people in two with his iron weapon and so escaped this onset, yet he saw nothing left behind of that appearingly divided body; at other times he outwrestled some of them. His neighbours often perceived this man to disappear at a certain place, and then about one hour after to become visible and discover himself near a bowshot from the first place. It was in that place where he became invisible, said he, that these subterraneans did encounter and combat with him. These who are unsained or unsanctified (called fey) are said to be *goinnt*, that is, pierced or wounded with those people's weapon, which makes them do somewhat very unlike their former practice, causing a sudden alteration, yet the cause thereof unperceivable at present. Nor have they power (either they cannot make use of their natural powers or ask not the heavenly aid) to escape the blow impendent. A man of the second sight perceived a person standing by him (sound to others' view) wholly gored in blood, and he, amazed-like, bid him instantly flee. The whole man laughed at his art and warning since there was no appearance of danger. He had scarce contracted his lips from laughter when unexpectedly his enemy leapt in at his side and stabbed him. With their weapons they also *gon*, or pierce, cows or other animals, usually said to be elf-shot, whose purest substance (if they die) these subterraneans take to live on, viz. the aerial and ethereal parts, the most spirituous matter for prolonging of life, such as aqua-vitae (moderately taken) is among liquors, leaving the terrestrial behind. The cure of such hurts is only for a man to find out the hole with his finger—as if the spirits flowing from a man's warm hand were antidote sufficient against their poisoned darts.

9. As birds and beasts, whose bodies are much used to the change of the free and open air, foresee storms, so those invisible people are more sagacious to understand by the Book of Nature things to come than we who are pestered with the grosser dregs of all elementary mixtures and have our purer spirits choked by them. The deer scents out a man and powder (though a late invention) at a great distance; a hungry hunter, bread; and the raven, a carrion: their brains being long clarified by the high and subtle air will observe a very small change in a trice. Thus a man of the second sight, perceiving the operations of these forecasting invisible people among us (indulged through a stupendous providence to give warnings of some remarkable events, either in the air, earth, or waters), told he saw a winding-shroud creep up on a walking healthful person's legs till it came to the knee, and afterwards it came up to the middle, then to the shoulders, and at last over the head, which was visible to no other person. And by observing the spaces of time betwixt the several stages, he easily guessed how long the man was to live who wore the shroud, for when it approached his head, he told that such a person was ripe for the grave.

10. There be many places called fairy-hills which the mountain-people think impious and dangerous to peel or discover by taking earth or wood from them, superstitiously believing the souls of their predecessors

to dwell there. And for that end (say they), a mote or mount was dedicate beside every churchyard to receive the souls, till their adjacent bodies arise, and so become as a fairy-hill, they using bodies of air when called abroad. They also affirm those creatures that move invisibly in a house, and cast huge great stones but do not much hurt (because counter-wrought by some more courteous and charitable spirits that are everywhere ready to defend men [Daniel 10.13]), to be souls that have not attained their rest through a vehement desire of revealing a murder or notable injury done or received, or a treasure that was forgot in their lifetime on earth, which when disclosed to a conjuror alone, the ghost quite removes.

In the next country to that of my former residence, about the year 1676, when there was some scarcity of grain, a marvellous illapse and vision strongly struck the imagination of two women in one night, living at a good distance from one another, about a treasure hid in a hill called *sith-bhruaich*, or fairy-hill. The appearance of a treasure was first represented to the fancy, and then an audible voice named the place where it was to their awaking senses. Whereupon both arose and, meeting accidentally at the place, discovered their design; and jointly digging found a vessel as large as a Scottish-peck, full of small pieces of good money, of ancient coin, which halving betwixt them they sold in dishfuls for dishfuls of meal to the country people.

Very many of undoubted credit saw and had of the coin to this day, but whether it was a good or bad angel, one of the subterranean people, or the restless soul of him who hid it that discovered it, and to what end it was done, I leave to the examination of others.

11. These subterraneans have controversies, doubts, disputes, feuds, and siding of parties, there being some ignorance in all creatures and the vastest created intelligences not compassing all things. As to vice and sin, whatever their own laws be, sure according to ours, and equity natural, civil, and revealed, they transgress and commit acts of injustice, and sin by what is above said as to their stealing of nurses to their children and that other sort of plaginism in catching our children away (may seem to heir some estate in those invisible dominions), which never return. For the incontinence of their *leannain sith*, or succubi, who tryst with men, it is abominable. But for swearing and intemperance, they are not observed so subject to those irregularities as to envy, spite, hypocrisy, lying, and dissimulation.

12. As our religion obliges us not to make a peremptory and curious search into these abstrusenesses, so the histories of all ages give as many plain examples of extraordinary occurrences as make a modest inquiry not contemptible. How much is written of pygmies,

fairies, nymphs, sirens, apparitions, which though not the tenth part true, yet could not spring of nothing? Even English authors relate of Barry Island in Glamorganshire that laying your ear unto a cleft of the rock, blowing of bellows, striking of hammers, clashing of armour, filing of irons will be heard distinctly, ever since Merlin enchanted those subterranean wights to a solid manual forging of arms to Aurelius Ambrosius and his Britains till he returned, which Merlin being killed in battle and not coming to loose the knot, these active Vulcans are there tied to a perpetual labour. But to dip no deeper into this well, I will next give some account how the seer, my informer, comes to have this secret way of correspondence beyond other mortals.

There be odd solemnities at investing a man with the privileges of the whole mystery of this second sight. He must run a tether of hair (which bound a corpse to the bier) in a helix about his middle from end to end, then bow his head downward (as did Elijah [I Kings 18.42]) and look back through his legs until he see a funeral advance till the people cross two marches, or look thus back through a hole where was a knot of fir. But if the wind change points while the hair-tether is tied about him he is in peril of his life. The usual method for a curious person to get a transient sight of this otherwise invisible crew of subterraneans (if importunately and over-rashly sought) is to put his foot on the seer's foot, and the seer's hand is put on the inquirer's head, who is to look over the wizard's right shoulder (which has an ill appearance, as if, by this ceremony, an implicit surrender were made of all betwixt the wizard's foot and his hand ere the person can be admitted a privado to the art). Then will he see a multitude of wights like furious hardy men flocking to him hastily from all quarters, as thick as atoms in the air, which are no nonentities or phantasms, creatures proceeding from an affrighted apprehension, confused or crazed sense, but realities, appearing to a stable man in his awaking sense and enduring a rational trial of their being. Those through fear strike him breathless and speechless, but the seer, defending the lawfulness of his skill, forbids such horror and comforts his novice by telling of Zacharias being struck speechless at seeing of apparitions (Luke 1.20). Then he further maintains his art by vouching Elisha to have the same and disclosed it thus unto his servant (in 2 Kings 6.17) when he blinded the Syrians, and Peter (in Acts 5.9) foreseeing the death of Sapphira by perceiving as it were her winding-sheet about her beforehand, and Paul (in 2 Corinthians 12.4), who got such a vision and sight as should not nor could be told. Elisha also in his chamber saw Gehazi his servant at a great distance taking a reward from Naaman (2 Kings 5.26). Hence were the prophets frequently called seers or men of a second and more exalted sight than others.

He cites for his purpose also Matthew 4.8, where the devil undertakes to give even Jesus a sight of all nations and the finest things in the world at one glance, though in their natural situations and stations at a vast distance from one another. And 'tis said expressly, he did let him see them, not in a map it seems, nor by a fantastic magical juggling of the sight, which he could not impose upon so discerning a person. It would appear then to have been a sight of real solid substances and things of worth which he intended as a bait for his purpose. Whence it might seem (comparing this relation of Matthew 4.8 with the former) that the extraordinary or second sight can be given by the ministry of bad as well as good spirits to those that will embrace it, and the instance of Balaam and the pythoness makes it nothing the less probable.

Thus also the seer trains his scholar by telling of the gradations of nature, ordered by a wise providence, that as the sight of bats and owls transcend that of shrews and moles, so the visive faculties of men are clearer than those of owls, as eagles', lynxes', and cats' are brighter than men's. And again that men of the second sight (being designed to give warnings against secret engines) surpass the ordinary vision of other men, which is a native habit in some, descended from their ancestors, and acquired as an artificial improvement of their natural sight in others, resembling in their own kind the usual artificial helps of optic glasses (as prospectives, telescopes, and microscopes). Without which adscititious aids, those men here treated of do perceive things that for their smallness or subtlety and secrecy are invisible to others, though daily conversant with them. They having such a beam continually about them, as that of the sun, which when it shines clear only lets common eyes see the atoms in the air that without these rays they could not discern. For some have this second sight transmitted from father to son through the whole family without their own consent or others' teaching, proceeding only from a bounty of providence, it seems, or by a compact or a complexional quality of the first acquirer (as it may seem alike strange (yet nothing vicious) in such as Mr. Greatrakes the Irish stroker, seventh sons, and others that cure the King's Evil, and chase away diseases and pains, with only stroking of the affected part). Which (if it be not the relics of miraculous operations or some secret virtue in the womb of the parent which increaseth until seven sons be born and decreaseth by the same degrees afterwards) proceeds only from the sanative balsam of their healthful constitutions, virtue going out from them by spirituous effluxes unto the patient, and their vigorous healthy spirits affecting the sick as usually the unhealthy fumes of the sick infect the sound and whole.

13. The minor sort of seers prognosticate many future events, only for a month's space, from the shoulderbone of a sheep on which a knife never came (for as before is said—and the Nazarites of old had something of it—iron hinders all the operations of those that travail in the intrigues of these hidden dominions). This science is called *slinnenacd*. By looking into the bone they will tell if whoredom be committed in the owner's house, what money the master of the sheep had, if any will die out of that house for that month, and if any cattle there will take a trake (as if planet-struck) called *earchall*. Then will they prescribe a preservative and prevention.

14. A woman (it seems, an exception from the general rule) singularly wise in these matters of foresight, living in Colonsay, an isle of the Hebrides (in time of the Marquis of Montrose, his wars with the states in Scotland), being notorious among many, and so examined by some that violently seized that isle, if she saw them coming or not, she said she saw them coming many hours before they came in view of the isle. But earnestly looking, she sometimes took them for enemies, sometimes for friends, and moreover they looked as if they went from the isle, not as men approaching it, which made her not put the inhabitants on their guard. The matter was that the barge wherein the enemy sailed was a little before taken from the inhabitants of that

same isle, and the men had their backs towards the isle when they were plying the oars towards it. Thus this old scout and Delphian Oracle was at last deceived and did deceive. Being asked who gave her such sights and warnings, she said that as soon as she set three crosses of straw upon the palm of her hand a great ugly beast sprang out of the earth near her and flew in the air. If what she enquired had success according to her wish, the beast would descend calmly and lick up the crosses. If it would not succeed, the beast would furiously thrust her and the crosses over on the ground and so vanish to his place.

15. Among other instances of undoubted verity proving *in thesi* the being of such aerial people or species of creatures not vulgarly known, I add these subsequent relations, some whereof I have from my acquaintance with the actors and patients, and the rest from eyewitnesses to the matter of fact. The first whereof shall be of a woman taken out of her child-bed and having a living image of her substituted in her room, which resemblance decayed, died, and was buried, but the person stolen returning to her husband after two years' space, he—being convinced by many undeniable tokens that she was his former wife—admitted her home and had divers children by her. Among other reports she gave her husband, this was one: that she perceived little what they did in the spacious house she lodged

in until she anointed one of her eyes with a certain unction that was by her, which they perceiving to have acquainted her with their actions, they fanned her blind of that eye with a puff of their breath. She found the place full of light, without any fountain or lamp from whence it did spring. This person lived in the country next to that of my last residence and might furnish matter of dispute among casuists, whether, if her husband had been married in the interim of her two years' absence, he was obliged to divorce from the second spouse at the return of the first. There is an art appearingly without superstition for recovering of such as are thus stolen, but I think it superfluous to insert it.

I saw a woman of forty years' age and examined her (having another clergyman in my company) about a report that passed of her long fasting—her name is NcIntyr. It was told by them of the house, as well as herself, that she took very little or no food for several years past, that she tarried in the fields overnight, saw and conversed with a people she knew not, having wandered in seeking of her sheep and slept upon a hillock, and finding herself transported to another place before day. The woman had a child since that time and is still pretty melancholious and silent, hardly ever seen to laugh. Her natural heat and radical moisture seem to be equally balanced, like an unextinguishable lamp, and going in a circle, not unlike to the faint life of bees and some sort of birds that sleep all the winter over and revive in the spring.

It is usual in all magical arts to have the candidates prepossessed with a belief of their tutor's skill and ability to perform their feats and act their juggling pranks and legerdemain; but a person called Stewart, possessed with a prejudice at all that was spoken of the second sight and living near to my house, was so put to it by a seer before many witnesses that he lost his speech and power of his legs and, breathing excessively as if expiring, because of the many fearful wights that appeared to him, the company were forced to carry him into the house.

It is notoriously known what in Killin within Perthshire fell tragically out with a yeoman that lived hard by, who coming to a company within an ale-house where a seer sat at table, that, at the sight of the entrant neighbour, the seer, starting, rose to go out of the house, and being asked the reason of his haste, told that the entrant man should die within two days, at which news the named entrant stabbed the seer and was himself executed two days after for the fact.

A minister, very intelligent but misbelieving all such sights as were not ordinary, chancing to be in a narrow lane with a seer, who perceiving a wight of a known visage furiously to encounter them, the seer desired the minister to turn out of the way, who scorning his reason and holding himself in the path with them when the seer was going hastily out of the way, they were both violently cast aside to a good distance, and the fall made them lame all their life. A little after the minister was carried home, one came to toll the bell for the death of the man whose representation met them in the narrow path some half an hour before.

Another example is a seer in Kentire in Scotland, sitting at table with divers others, suddenly did cast his head aside; the company asking why he did it, he answered that such a friend of his, by name, then in Ireland, threatened immediately to cast a dishful of butter in his face. The men wrote down the day and hour and sent to the gentleman to know the truth, which deed the gentleman declared he did at that very time, for he knew that his friend was a seer and would make sport with it. The men that were present and examined the matter exactly told me this story and withal that a seer would, with all his optics, perceive no other object so readily as this at such a distance.

A succinct account of My Lord of Tarbat's relations in a letter to the Honorable Robert Boyle, Esquire (of the predictions made by seers whereof himself was ear- and eyewitness) I thought fit to adjoin hereunto, that I might not be thought singular in this disquisition, that the matter of fact might be undeniably made out, and that I might with all submission give some annotations, with animadversions on his supposed causes of that phenomenon, with my reasons of dissent from his judgment:

Sir,

I heard very much but believed very little of the second sight, yet its being affirmed by severals of great veracity, I was induced to make inquiry after it in the year 1652, being then confined to abide in the North of Scotland by the English usurpers. The more general accounts of it were that many Highlanders, yet far more Islanders, were qualified with this second sight. That men, women, and children indistinctly were subject to it, and children where parents were not. Sometimes people came to age who had it not when young, nor could any tell by what means produced. It is a trouble to most of them who are subject to it, and they would be rid of it at any rate if they could. The sight is no long duration, only continuing so long as they can keep their eye steady without twinkling. The hardy therefore fix their look that they may see the longer. But the timorous see only glances, their eyes always twinkling at the first sight of the object.

That which generally is seen by them are the species of living creatures and of animate things which are in motion, such as ships and habits upon persons. They never see the species of any person who is already dead. What they foresee fails not to exist in the mode and in that place where it appears to them. They cannot well know what space of time shall intervene between the apparition and the real existence. But some of the hardiest and longest experience have some rules for conjectures as: if they see a man with a shrouding sheet in the apparition, they will conjecture at the nearness or remoteness of his death by the more or less of his body that is covered by it; they will ordinarily see their absent friends, though at a great distance —sometimes no less than from America to Scotland— sitting, standing, or walking in some certain place, and then they conclude with assurance that they will see them so and there; if a man be in love with a woman, they will ordinarily see the species of that man standing by her, and so likewise if a woman be in love, and they conjecture at their enjoyments (of each other) by the species touching the person or appearing at a distance from her (if they enjoy not one another). If they see the species of any person who is sick to die, they see them covered over with the shrouding sheet.

These generals I had verified to me by such of them as did see and were esteemed honest and sober by all the neighbourhood. For I inquired after such for my information. And because there were more of these seers in the Isles of Lewis, Harris, and Uist than in any other place, I did entreat Sir James Mcdonald (who is now dead), Sir Norman Macleod, and Mr. Daniel Morison, a very honest parson, (who are still alive) to make inquiry in this uncouth sight and to acquaint me therewith, which they did, and all found an agreement in these generals and informed me of many instances confirming what they said. But though men of discretion and honour, being but at second hand, I will choose rather to put myself than my friends on the hazard of being laughed at for incredible relations.

I was once travelling in the Highlands and a good number of servants with me, as is usual there, and one of them going a little before me, entering into a house where I was to stay all night, and going hastily to the door, he suddenly stepped back with a screech and did fall by a stone which hit his foot. I asked what the matter was, for he seemed to be very much frightened. He told me very seriously that I should not lodge in that house, because shortly a dead coffin would be carried out of it, for many were carrying of it when he was heard cry. I, neglecting his words and staying there, he said to other of the servants he was sorry for it and that surely what he saw would shortly come to pass, though no sick person was then there. Yet the landlord, a healthy Highlander, died of an apoplectic fit before I left the house.

In the year of 1653, Alexander Munro (afterward Lieutenant Colonel to the Earl of Dumbarton's Regiment) and I were walking in a place called Ullapool in Loch Broom on a little plain at the foot of a rugged hill, where was a servant working with a spade in the walk before us; his back was to us and his face to the hill. Before we came near to him he let the spade fall and looked toward the hill. He took notice of us as we passed nearby him, which made me look at him, and perceiving him to stare a little strangely, I conjectured him to be a seer. I called at him, at which he started and smiled. "What are you doing?" said I. He answered, "I have seen a very strange thing, an army of Englishmen leading of horses coming down that hill, and a number of them are come down to the plain and eating the barley which is growing in the field near to the hill." This was on the fourth of May (for I noted the day) and it was four or five days before the barley was sown in the field he spoke of. Alexander Munro asked him how he knew they were Englishmen. He said, "Because they were leading of horses and had on hats and boots," which he knew no Scotchman would have there. We took little notice of the whole story as other than a foolish vision, but wished that an English party were there, we being then at war with them and the place almost inaccessible for horsemen. But in the beginning of August thereafter, the Earl of Middleton (then Lieutenant for the King in the Highlands), having occasion to march a party of his toward the South Highlands, he sent his foot through a place called Inverlael, and the fore-party which was first down the hill did fall of eating the barley which was on the little plain under it, and Munro calling to mind what the seer told us in May preceding, he wrote of it, and sent an express to me to Lochslin in Ross (where I then was) with it.

I had occasion once to be in company where a young lady was (excuse my not naming of persons) and I was told there was a notable seer in the company. I called him to speak with me, as I did ordinarily when I found any of them, and after he had answered me to several questions, I asked if he knew any person to be in love with that lady. He said he did, but he knew not the person, for during the two days he had been in her company, he perceived one standing near her and his head leaning on her shoulder, which (he said) did foretell that the man should marry her and die before her (according to his observation). This was in the year 1655. I desired him to describe the person, which he did, so that I could conjecture by the description of such a one who was of that lady's acquaintance, though there were no thought of their marriage till two years thereafter.

And having occasion in the year 1657 to find this seer, who was an Islander, in company with the other person whom I conjectured to have been described by him, I called him aside and asked if that was the person he saw beside the lady near two years past. He said it was he indeed, for he had seen that lady just then standing by him hand in hand. This was some few months before their marriage, and the man is since dead and the lady still alive.

I shall trouble you but with one more which I thought most remarkable of any that occurred to me. In January 1652 the above mentioned Lieutenant Colonel Alexander Munro and I happened to be in the house of one William McLeud of Farranlea in the county of Ross. He, the landlord, and I were sitting in three chairs near the fire, and in the corner of the great chimney there were two Islanders, who were that very night come to the house and were related to the landlord. While the one of them was talking with Munro, I perceived the other to look oddly toward me; from this look and his being an Islander, I conjectured him a seer and asked him at what he stared. He answered by desiring me to rise from that chair, for it was an unlucky one. I asked why. He answered, because there was a dead man in the chair next to me. "Well," said I, "if it be in the next chair, I may keep my own. But what is the likeness of the man?" He said he was a tall man with a long gray coat, booted, and one of his legs hanging over the arm of the chair, and his head hanging dead to the other side, and his arm backward, as if it was broken.

There were some English troops then quartered near that place, and (there being at that time a great frost after a thaw) the country was covered all over with ice. Four or five of the English riding by this house some two hours after the vision, while we were sitting by the fire, we heard a great noise which proved to be these troopers, with the help of other servants, carrying in one of their number, who had got a very mischievous fall and had his arm broke, and falling frequently in swooning fits. They brought into the hall and set him in the very chair and in the very posture that the seer had proposed, but the man did not die, though he recovered with great difficulty.

Among the accounts given me by Sir Norman Macleod, there was one worthy of special notice, which was thus. There was a gentleman in the Isle of Harris who was always seen by the seers with an arrow in his thigh. Such in the Isle who thought those prognostications infallible did not doubt but that he would be shot in the thigh before he died. Sir Norman told me that he heard it the subject of their discourse for many years when that gentleman was present. At last he died without any such accident. Sir Norman was at his burial at Saint Clement's Church in the Harris. At the same time the corpse of another gentleman was brought to be buried in the same very church. The friends on either side came to debate who should first enter the church, and in a trice from words they came to blows. One of the number (who was armed with bow and arrows) let one fly among them. (Now every family in that isle have their burial-place in the church in stone chests, and the bodies are carried in open biers to the burial-place.) Sir Norman having appeased the tumult, one of the arrows was found shot in the dead man's thigh. To this Sir Norman himself was a witness.

In the account which Mr. Daniel Morison, parson in the Lewis, gave me, there was one which, though it be heterogeneous from this subject, yet it may be worth your notice. It was of a young woman in his parish who was mightily frightened by seeing her own image still before her, always when she came into the open air, the back of the image being always to her, so that it was not a reflection as in a mirror but the species of such a body as her own, and in a very like habit, which appeared to herself continually before her. The parson kept her a long while with him but had no remedy of her evil, which troubled her exceedingly. I was told afterwards that when she was four or five years elder she saw it not.

These are matters of fact, which I assure you are truly related. But those and all others that occurred to me, by information or otherwise, could never lead me into a remote conjecture of the cause of so extraordinary a phenomenon. Whether it be a quality in the eyes of some people in those parts, concurring with a quality in the air also; whether such species be everywhere, though not seen by the want of eyes so qualified, or from whatever other cause; I must leave to the enquiry of clearer judgments than mine. But a hint may be taken from this image, which appeared still to this woman above-mentioned, and from another mentioned by Aristotle in the fourth of his *Metaphysics*, if I remember right (for it is long since I read it), as also from that common opinion that young infants (unsullied with many objects) do see apparitions which are not seen by those of elder years, as likewise from this, that several did see the second sight when in the Highlands or Isles, yet when transported to live in other countries, especially in America, they quite lost this quality, as was told me by a gentleman who knew some of them in Barbados who did see no vision there, although he knew them to be seers when they lived in the Isles of Scotland.

Thus far My Lord Tarbat.

———

My Lord, after narrow inquisition, hath delivered many true and remarkable observations on this subject, yet to encourage a further scrutiny I crave leave to say that:

1. But a few women are endowed with this sight in respect of men, and their predictions not so certain.

2. This sight is not criminal, since a man can come by it unawares and without his consent. But it is certain he see more fatal and fearful things than he do gladsome.

3. The seers avouch that several who go to the *siths*

(or people at rest and, in respect of us, in peace) before the natural period of their lives expire do frequently appear to them.

4. A vehement desire to attain this art is very helpful to the inquirer, and the species of an absent friend, which appears to the seer as clearly as if he had sent his lively picture to present itself before him, is no fantastic shadow of a sick apprehension but a reality and a messenger coming for unknown reasons, not from the original similitude of itself but from a more swift and pragmatic people, which recreate themselves in offering secret intelligence to men, though generally they are unacquainted with that kind of correspondence, as if they lived in a different element from them.

5. Though my collections were written long before I saw My Lord of Tarbat, yet I am glad that his descriptions and mine correspond so nearly. The maid My Lord mentions who saw her image still before her suiteth with the co-walker named in my account. Which, though some at first thought might conjecture to be by the refraction of a cloud or mist, as in the *parelii* (the whole air and every drop of water being a mirror to return the species of things, were our visive faculty sharp enough to apprehend them), or a natural reflection from the same reasons that an echo can be redoubled by art, yet it were more feasible to impute this second sight to a quality infused into the eye by an unction (for witches have a sleepy ointment that,

when applied, troubles their fantasy, advancing it to have unusual figures and shapes represented to it, as if it were a fit of fanaticism, hypochondriac melancholy, or possession of some insinuating spirit raising the soul beyond its common strain), if the palpable instants and realities seen and innocently objected to the senses did not disprove it and make the matter a palpable verity and no deception. Yet since this sight can be bestowed without ointment or dangerous compact, the qualification is not of so bad an original. Therefore,

6. By My Lord's good leave, I presume to say that this sight can be no quality of the air nor of the eyes. Because: (i) such as live in the same air and see all other things as far off and as clearly, yet have not the second sight; (ii) a seer can give another person this sight transiently by putting his hand and foot in the posture he requires of him; (iii) the unsullied eyes of infants can naturally perceive no new unaccustomed objects but what appear to other men, unless exalted and clarified some way, as Balaam's ass for a time (though in a witch's eye the beholder cannot see his own image reflected, as in the eyes of other people), so that defect of objects, as well as diversity of the subject, may operate differently on several tempers and ages; (iv) though also some are of so venomous a constitution, by being radicated in envy and malice, that they pierce and kill (like a cockatrice) whatever creature they first set their eye on in the morning, so was it

with Walter Graham, sometime living in the same parish wherein now I am, who killed his own cow after commending its fatness and shot a hare with his eye, having praised its swiftness, such was the infection of an evil eye, albeit this was unusual, yet he saw no object but what was obvious to other men as well as to himself; (v) if the being transported to live in another country did obscure the second sight, neither the parson nor the maid needed be much troubled for her reflex-self, a little peregrination and going from her wonted home would have salved her fear. Wherefore,

7. Since the things seen by the seers are real entities, the presages and predictions found true, but a few endowed with this sight and those not of bad lives or addicted to malefices, the true solution of the phenomenon seems rather to be the courteous endeavours of our fellow creatures in the invisible world to convince us (in opposition to Sadducees, Socinians, and Atheists) of a deity, of spirits, of a possible and harmless method of correspondence betwixt men and them even in this life, of their operations for our caution and warning, of the orders and degrees of angels, whereof one order with bodies of air condensed and curiously shaped may be next to man, superior to him in understanding yet unconfirmed, and of their region habitation and influences on man, greater than that of stars on inanimate bodies—a knowledge (belike) reserved for these last Atheistic ages, wherein the

profanity of men's lives hath debauched and blinded their understandings as to Moses, Jesus, and the prophets (unless they get convictions from things formerly known) as from the regions of the dead.

Nor doth the ceasing of the visions upon the seer's transmigration into foreign kingdoms make His Lordship's conjecture of the quality of the air and eye a whit the more probable, but on the contrary it confirms greatly my account of an invisible people, guardian over and careful of men, who have their different offices and abilities in distant countries, as appears in Daniel 10.13, etc. Israel's, Grecia's, and Persia's assistant princes, whereof who so prevaileth, give the dominion and ascendant to his pupils (and vassals over the opposite armies and countries), so that every country and kingdom having their topical spirits or powers assisting and governing them, the Scottish seer banished to America, being a stranger there as well to the invisible as to the visible inhabitants and wanting the familiarity of his former correspondents, he could not have the favour and warnings by the several visions and predictions which were wont to be granted him by those acquaintances and favourites in his own country. For if what he wont to see were realities (as I have made appear), 'twere too great an honour for Scotland to have such seldom-seen watchers and predominant powers over it alone, acting in it so expressly, and all other nations wholly destitute of the like; though without all peradventure all other people wanted the right key of their cabinet and the exact method of correspondence with them, except the sagacious active Scots, a many of whom have retained it of a long time and by surprises and raptures do often foretell what in kindness is really represented to them at several occasions.

To which purpose the learned lynx-eyed Mr. Baxter on Revelation 12.7, writing of the fight betwixt Michael and the Dragon, gives a very pertinent note, viz. that he knows not but ere any great action (especially tragical) is done on earth, that first the battle and victory is acted and achieved in the air betwixt the good and evil spirits (thus he). It seems these were the men's guardians, and the like battles are ofttimes perceived aloft in the night time, the event of which might easily be represented by some one of the number to a correspondent on earth, as frequently the report of great actions hath been more swiftly carried to other countries than all the art of us mortals could possibly dispatch it. Saint Augustine on Mark 9.4 giveth no small intimation of this truth, averring that Elias appeared with Jesus on the Mount in his proper body, but Moses in an aerial body, assumed like the angels who appeared, and had ability to eat with Abraham, though no necessity, on the account of their bodies, as likewise the late doctrine of the pre-existence of souls living into aerial vehicles, gives a singular hint of the possibility of the thing if not a direct proof of the whole assertion; which yet moreover may be illuminated by divers other instances of the like nature and as wonderful, besides what is above said as:

8. The invisible wights which haunt houses seem rather to be some of our subterranean inhabitants (which appear often to men of the second sight) than evil spirits or devils, because though they throw great stones, pieces of earth, and wood at the inhabitants, they hurt them not at all, as if they acted not maliciously like devils but in sport like buffoons and drolls. All ages have afforded some obscure testimonies of it, as Pythagoras, his doctrine of transmigration; Socrates's Daemon that gave him precautions of future dangers; Plato's classing them into various vehiculated species of spirits; Dionysius Areopagitica's marshalling nine orders of spirits superior and subordinate; the poets their borrowing of the philosophers and adding their own fancies of fountain, river, and sea nymphs, wood, hill, and mountain inhabitants, and that every place and thing in cities and countries had special invisible regular gods and governors. Cardano speaks of his father, his seeing the species of his friend in a moonshine night riding fiercely by his window on a white horse the very night his friend died at a vast distance from him, by which he understood that some alteration would suddenly ensue. Cornelius Agrippa and the learned Dr. More have several passages tending that way. The noctambulos themselves would ap-

pear to have some foreign joking spirit possessing and supporting them when they walk on deep waters and tops of houses without danger when asleep and in the dark. For it is no way probable that mere apprehension and strange imagination, setting the animal spirits awork to move the body, could preserve it from sinking in the depths or falling down headlong when asleep anymore than when awake, the body being then as ponderous as before; and it is hard to attribute it to a spirit flatly evil and enemy to man, because the noctambulo returns to his own place safe. And the most furious tribe of the daemons are not permitted by providence to attack men so frequently either by night or by day: for in our Highlands, as there be many fair ladies of this aerial order which do often tryst with lascivious young men in the quality of succubi or lightsome paramours and strumpets (called *leannain sith*, or familiar spirits in Deuteronomy 18.11), so do many of our Highlanders (as if astrangling by the nightmare, pressed with a fearful dream, or rather possessed by one of our aerial neighbours) rise up fiercely in the night and, apprehending the nearest weapons, push and thrust at all persons in the same room with them, sometimes wounding their own comrades to dead, the like whereof fell sadly out within a few miles of me at the writing hereof.

I add but one instance more of a very young maid who lived near to my last residence, that in one night learned a large piece of poesy by the frequent repetition of it from one of our nimble and courteous spirits, whereof a part was pious, the rest superstitious (for I have a copy of it). But no other person were ever heard to repeat it before, nor was the maid capable to compose it of herself.

9. Having demonstrated and made evident to sense this extraordinary vision of our tramontane seers and what is seen by them by what is said above (many having seen this same spectres and apparitions at once, having their visive faculties entire, for *non est disputandum de gustibus*), it now remains to show that it is not unsuitable to reason nor the Holy Scriptures. (i) First, that it's not repugnant to reason doth appear from this: that it is no less strange for immortal sparks and souls to come and be immersed into gross terrestrial elementary bodies and be so propagated, so nourished, so fed, so clothed as they are, and breathe in such an air and world prepared for them, than for Hollanders, or hollow-cavern inhabitants, to live and traffic amongst us in another state of being without our knowledge; for Raymond Sebond, in his Third Book, Chapter 12, argues quaintly that all sorts of living creatures have a happy rational polity of their own with great contentment, which government and mutual converse of theirs they all pride and plume themselves, because it is as unknown to man as man's is to them; much more, that the Son of the Highest Spirit should as-

sume a body like ours convinces all the world that no other thing that is possible needs be much wondered at. (ii) The manucodiata, or bird of paradise, living in the highest region of the air; common birds in the second region; flies and insects in the lowest; men and beasts on earth's surface; worms, otters, badgers, and fishes under the earth and waters; likewise Hell is inhabited at the centre and Heaven in the circumference—can we then think the middle cavities of the earth empty? I have seen in Wemyss (a place in the county of Fyfe in Scotland) divers caves cut out as vast temples under ground; the like is in a county of England. In Malta is a cave wherein stones of a curious cut are thrown in great numbers every day. So I have had barbed arrowheads of yellow flint that could not be cut so small and neat, of so brittle a substance, by all the art of man. It would seem therefore that these mentioned works were done by certain spirits of pure organs and not by devils, whose continual torments could not allow them so much leisure.

Besides these, I have found five curiosities in Scotland, not much observed to be elsewhere: (i) the brownies, who in some families as drudges clean the houses and dishes after all go to bed, taking with him his portion of food and removing before daybreak; (ii) the Mason Word which, though some make a mystery of it, I will not conceal a little of what I know—it's like a rabbinical tradition in a way of comment on Jachin and Boaz, the two pillars erected in Solomon's Temple, with an addition of some secret sign delivered from hand to hand by which they know and become familiar one with another; (iii) this second sight so largely treated of before; (iv) charms and curing (by them) very many diseases, sometimes by transferring the sickness to another; (v) a being proof of lead, iron, and silver, or a brieve making men invulnerable—divers of our Scottish commanders and soldiers have been seen with blue marks only, after they were shot with leaden ball, which seems to be an Italian trick, for they seem to be a people too curious and magically inclined.

Finally, Irishmen, our Northern Scottish, and our Atholl men are so much addicted to and delighteth with harps and music as if, like King Saul, they were possessed with a foreign spirit, only with this difference: that music did put Saul's play-fellow asleep but roused and awaked our men, vanquishing their own spirits at pleasure, as if they were impotent of its powers and unable to command it, for we have seen some poor beggars of them chattering their teeth for cold, that how soon they saw the fire and heard the harp, leapt through the house like goats and satyrs.

As there are parallel stories in all countries and ages reported of these our obscure people (which are no dotages), so it is no more of necessity to us fully to know their beings and manner of life than to understand distinctly the polity of the nine orders of angels;

or with what oil the lamp of the sun is maintained so long and regularly; or why the moon is called a great luminary in Scripture, while it only appears to be so; or if the moon be truly inhabited because telescopes discover seas and mountains in it, as well as flaming furnaces in the sun; or why the discovery of America was looked on as a fairy tale and the reporters hooted at as inventers of ridiculous utopias, or the first probable asserters punished as inventers of new gods and worlds; or why in England the King cures the struma by stroking, and the seventh son in Scotland, whether his temperate complexion conveys a balsam and sucks out the corrupting principles by a frequent warm sanative contact; or whether the parents of the seventh child put forth a more eminent virtue to his production than to all the rest, as being the αχμη, meridian, and height to which their vigour ascends and from that forth have a gradual declining into a feebleness of the body and its productions. And then: (i) Why is not the seventh son infected himself by that contagion he extracts from another? (ii) How can once or twice stroking with a cold hand have so strong a natural operation as to exhale all the infectious worming, corroding vapours? (iii) Why may not a seventh daughter have the same virtue? So that it appears, albeit a happy natural constitution concur, yet something is in it above nature.

Therefore every age hath some secret left for its discovery, and who knows but this intercourse betwixt the two kinds of rational inhabitants of the same earth may be not only believed shortly but as freely entertained and as well known as now the art of navigation, printing, gunning, riding on saddles with stirrups, and the discoveries of microscopes which were sometimes as great a wonder and as hard to be believed.

10. Though I will not be so curious nor so peremptory as he who will prove the possibility of the philosopher's stone from Scripture (Job 28.1.2; Job 22.24.25), nor the plurality of worlds from John 14.2 and Hebrews 11.3, nor the circulation of the blood from Ecclesiastes 12.6, nor the talismanical art from the blind and lame mentioned in 2 Samuel 5.6, yet I humbly propose these passages which may give some light to our subject at least and show that this polity and rank of people is not a thing impossible, nor the modest and innocent scrutiny of them impertinent or unsafe. The legion or brigade of spirits (mentioned in Mark 5.10) besought our Saviour not to send them away out of that country, which shows they were *daemones loci* (topical spirits) and peculiar superintendents and supervisors assigned to that province, and the power of the nations granted [Revelation 2.26] to the conquerors of vice and infidelity sound somewhat to that purpose. Tobit had a daemon attending marriage, (Tobit 3.8), and in Matthew 4.5 an evil spirit came in a visible shape to tempt our Saviour, who himself denied not the sensible appearing of ghosts to our sight, but

said their bodies were not composed of flesh and bones as ours (Luke 24.39), and in Philippians 2.10 our very subterraneans are expressly said to bow to the name of Jesus. Elisha, not intellectually only but sensibly, saw Gehazi when out of the reach of an ordinary view. It wants not good evidence that there are more managed by God's spirit—good, evil, and intermediate spirits— among men in this world than we are aware of, the good spirits ingesting fair and heroic apprehensions and images of virtue and the divine life, thereby animating us to act for a higher happiness according to our improvement and relinquishing us as strangely upon our neglect or our embracing the deceitful siren-like pictures and representations of pleasures and gain presented to our imaginations by evil and sportful angels to allure us to an unthinking, ungenerous, and sensual life, none of them having power to compel us to any misdemeanour without our flat consent. Moreover, this life of ours being called a warfare, and God's saying that at last there will be no peace to the wicked; our busy and silent companions also being called *siths*, or people at rest and quiet in respect of us; and withal many ghosts appearing to men that want this second sight, in the very shapes and speaking the same language they did when incorporate and alive with us, a matter that is of an old imprescriptable tradition (our Highlanders making still a distinction betwixt *sluagh saoghalta* and *sluagh sith*, averring that the souls go to the *sith* when dislodged); many real treasures and murders being discovered by souls that pass from among ourselves or by the kindness of these our airy neighbours (none of which spirits can be altogether inorganical), no less than the conceits about Purgatory, or a state of rescue, the *limbus patrum*, and *infantum*, inventions though misapplied, yet are not chimeras and altogether groundless, for *ab origine* it is nothing but some blanch and faint discoveries of this secret republic of ours here treated on; and additional fictions of monks' doting and crazy heads; our creed saying that our Saviour descended ʽεις αδμην to the invisible place and people; and many divines supposing that the Deity appeared in a visible shape seen by Adam in the cool of the day and speaking to him with an audible voice; and Jesus probably by the ministry of invisible attendants conveying more meat of the same kind to the five thousand that was fed by him with a very few loaves and fishes (for a new creation it was not); the zijim jiim and ochim in Isaiah 13.21–22 (those "satyrs and doleful unknown creatures of islands and deserts" seem to have a plain prospect that way); finally, the eternal happiness enjoyed in the third Heavens being more mysterious than most of men take it to be: it is not a sense wholly adduced to Scripture to say that this second sight and the due objects of it hath some vestige in Holy Writ, but rather 'tis modestly deduced from it.

II.

It only now remains to answer the most obvious objections against the reality and lawfulness of this speculation as:

QUESTION 1: How do you salve this second sight from compact and witchcraft?

ANSWER: Though this correspondence with the intermediate unconfirmed people (betwixt man and angel) be not ordinary to all of us who are superterraneans, yet this sight falling to some persons by accident and it being connatural to others from their birth, the derivation of it cannot always be wicked. A too great curiosity indeed to acquire an unnecessary art may be blameworthy, but divers of that secret commonwealth may by permission discover themselves as innocently to us, who are in another state, as some of us men do to fishes, which are in another element, when we plunge and dive into the bottom of the seas, their native region; and in process of time, we may come to converse as familiarly with those nimble and agile clans (but with greater pleasure and profit) as we do now with the Chinese and Antipodes.

QUESTION 2: Are they subject to vice, lusts, passion, and injustice as we who live on the surface of the earth?

ANSWER: The seers tell us that these wandering aerial people have not such an impetus and fatal tendency to any vice as men, as not being drenched into so gross and dreggy bodies as we, but yet are in an imperfect state, and some of them making better essays for heroic actions than others, having the same measures of virtue and vice as we, and still expecting advancement to a higher and more splendid state of life. One of them is stronger than many men, yet do not incline to hurt mankind, except by commission for a gross misdemeanour, as the destroying angel of Egypt and the Assyrians (Exodus 12.29, 2 Kings 19.35). They haunt most where is most barbarity, and therefore our ignorant ancestors to prevent the insults of that strange people used as rude and coarse a remedy, such as exorcisms, donations, and vows: but how soon ever true piety prevailed in any place, it did put the inhabitants beyond the reach and authority of those subtle inferior cohabitants and colleagues of ours; the Father of all Spirits and the person himself having the only command of his soul and actions. A concurrence they have to what is virtuously done, for upon committing of a foul deed, one will find a demur upon his soul, as if his cheerful colleague had deserted him.

QUESTION 3: Do these airy tribes procreate? If so, how are they nourished and at what period of time do they die?

ANSWER: Supposing all spirits to be created at once in the beginning, souls to pre-exist, and to circle about into several states of probationship to make them either totally unexcusable or perfectly happy against the last day, salves all the difficulty; but in every deed, and speaking suitable to the nature of things, there is no more absurdity for a spirit to inform an infantine body of air than a body composed of dull and drowsy earth, the best of spirits having always delighted more to appear into aerial than into terrestrial bodies. They feed mostwhat on quintessences and ethereal essences; the pith and spirits only of women's milk feed their children, being artificially conveyed (as air and oil sink into our bodies) to make them vigorous and fresh. And this shorter way of conveying a pure aliment (without the usual digestions), by transfusing it and transpiring through the pores into the veins and arteries and vessels that supply the body, is nothing more absurd than an infant's being fed by the navel before it is born, or than a plant which groweth by attracting a lively juice from the earth through many small roots and tendons (whose coarser parts being adapted and made connatural to the whole, doth quickly coalesce by the ambient cold), and so are condensed and baked up into a confirmed wood in the one and solid body of flesh and bone in the other—a notion which if entertained and approved may show that the late invention of soaking and transfusing not blood, but ethereal virtual spirits may be useful both for nourishment and health, whereof there is a vestige in the damnable practice of evil angels, their sucking of blood and spirits out of witches' bodies (till they drain them into a deformed and dry leanness) to feed their own vehicles withal, leaving what we call the witches' mark behind (a spot that I have seen as a small mole, horny and brown coloured, through which mark, when a large brass pin was thrust—both in buttock, nose, and roof of the mouth—till it bowed and became crooked, the witches, both men and women, neither felt a pain nor did bleed, nor knew the precise time when this was a doing to them [their eyes only being covered]). Now the air being a body as well as earth, no reason can be given why there may not be particles of more vivific spirit formed of it for procreation than is possible to be of earth, which takes more time and pains to rarify and ripen it ere it can come to have a prolific virtue, and if our tripping darlings did not thus procreate, their whole number would be exhausted after a considerable space of time. For though they are of more refined bodies and intellectuals than we, and of far less heavy and corruptive humours (which cause a dissolution), yet many of their lives being dissonant to right reason and their own laws and their vehicles not being wholly free of lust and passion, especially of the more spiritual and haughty sins, they pass (after a long healthy life) into an orb and receptacle fitted for their degree till they come under the general cognizance of the last day.

QUESTION 4: Doth the acquiring of this second

sight make any change on the acquirer's body, mind, or actions?

ANSWER: All uncouth sights enfeebles the seer. Daniel though familiar with divine visions, yet fell frequently down without strength when dazzled with a power which had the ascendant of and pressed on him beyond his comprehension (Daniel 10.8–17). So our seer is put in a rapture, transport, and sort of death, as divested of his body and all its senses, when he is first made participant of this curious piece of knowledge. But it maketh no wramp or strain in the understanding of any—only to the fancies of clownish and illiterate men it creates some affrightments and disturbances, because of the strangeness of the shows and their unacquaintedness with them. And as for the life, the persons endowed with this rarity are for the most part candid, honest, and sociable people. If any of them be subject to immoralities, this abstruse skill is not to be blamed for it, for unless themselves be the tempters, the colonies of the invisible plantations with which they intercommune do provoke them to no villainy or malefice, neither at their first acquaintance nor after a long familiarity.

QUESTION 5: Doth not Satan interpose in such cases by many subtle, unthought-of insinuations, as to him who let the fly or familiar go out of the box, and yet found the fly of his own putting-in as serviceable as the other would have been?

ANSWER: The goodness of the life and designs of the ancient prophets and seers was one of the best proofs of their mission. Nor have our seers bad lives and designs as necromancers and those that traffic with devils usually have: our seers moreover do seldom perform any odd thing themselves, but see what is done by others, which if acted by spirits flatly evil, their aim could not but appear by some extravagant work or malefice of the seers. Yet it is well known everywhere that our seers are no way scandalous men.

OBJECTION 6: This second sight was not an art or faculty in use or of good fame among men, or recommended of God.

ANSWER: Every unusual art or science is not sinful or unlawful, unless its original or principal design do make it so; nor was God always pleased to discover even every necessary truth at once, yet when such truths and sciences were permitted, recommended, or suggested, they were truly lawful: it was a long time before the Jews thought it lawful to war on the Lord's day, and the religious Jews themselves were long without a distinct knowledge of the Son of God and of the Holy Ghost —yet because of the noble design of that discovery, it ought not to be rejected when furder revived.

OBJECTION 7: If it was not diabolic, it is no reality, but apprehension.

ANSWER: That this species of vision is real and not fantastic is evident from the inquirer's conviction of the truth of it, though he come to the seer possessed with prejudice and with a previous misbelief of the art (which qualification usually mars the effort of all juggling and deceitful tricks). Not to say that the alleged *Speculum Trinitatis* by which every creature is seen in the Divine Essence, which some call the beatific vision, gives some light and probability to this branch or beam of vision, sure Elisha's servant having his eyes opened (2 Kings 6.17) and seeing the mountains full of horses and chariots of the heavenly host shows that there is a sight beyond ordinary acquirable even on earth, by infusing some quality in the eye, and that intelligences traverse daily among us on earth, directing, warning, or encamping about the faithful, though unknown and unseen to most men that live on it.

OBJECTION 8: The having of the second sight, though from the parents, being a voluntary act, and having no natural dependence of cause and effect, it is therefore sinful. The curious desire to know it, or put it in practice, being a believing of the art and trusting to it, is an unusual gift, magical, not from the beginning, and hath neither a precept of God in Scripture, nor promise of blessing in the exercise.

ANSWER: To those children on whom the second sight descends from their parents it is no voluntary act, but forced on them. And as for a dependence betwixt cause and effect, the cure of the King's Evil by the King from his ancestors (Edward the Saint downwards) and always by the seventh son is a real effect but depends not upon a natural cause known to us—and yet it is not scandalous nor sinful. Yawning is voluntary yet affecteth others by imitation, and doth it innocently; so doth the lodestone attract steel necessarily. But we know not the dependence of these effects from their natural causes, yet are they either harmless in themselves or profitable. For trusting to the art and believing of it, the seers cannot but believe there is such an art when many infallible instances presented to their sense do convince them of the reality; and yet they do not trust to it, for they for most part neither seek to the art nor expect any advantage or pleasure by it either in way of enriching themselves or revengement on others. And further, a person may be sinfully curious of a real and honest art which yet by accident (being useless and spending too much time) may become sinful to him. As to a promise of blessing upon having the sight, it not being an article of faith, a matter of salvation, or necessity, but only as another art or science lately invented (which shortly may become a profitable and pleasant speculation), it needs no more an express precept or promise than many other laudable actions and contemplations, undoubtedly, providing our belief be firm and our actions otherwise virtuous and devout. It could not endanger our salvation though we knew not that there were such things in the universe as a crew of infernal malicious devils, yet 'tis many ways profitable for us to know so much, which is pat and exactly applicable to our present case as to our conjunct inhabitants of this earthly footstool.

OBJECTION 9: That the proceeding from their fore-fathers did not diminish the sin or scandal of the second sight, more than original sin and other voluntary sins (as well as those of ignorance) are innocently derived from our progenitors.

ANSWER: Albeit original sin and its fatal consequence be not innocently derived to us from our progenitors, because of his Maker's covenant with Adam for himself and his posterity as to standing or falling, yet this doth not make hereditary diseases and all other things of our immediate parents sinfully to affect us. It might have been a sin of intemperance and riot in the parents that entailed a radicated inveterate distemper and bodily disease in the progeny, which yet is not the sin, but affliction of the children. It is the nature of the thing itself in question, and not the manner of its derivation and other accidental concomitants, which makes it faulty. If parents had this second sight by contract with evil spirits, it were error on the first concoction, which would still increase as it proceeded forward among their succession. But by undeniable proofs above, I have made it appear that both young children and aged persons have had this sight infused in a trice, they know not whence, though they neither concurred to it themselves, nor any of their parents and other

relations had the like before them—so that the spies
and aerial intelligent creatures and the sight of the
seers of them, clear and lawful and void of deception:
Quod erat demonstrandum.

CONCLUSION

Thus far of the lychnobious people, their nature, constitutions, actions, apparel, language, armour, and religion, with the quality of those amphibious seers that
correspond with them. For what is said of their procreation among themselves, which is done at the consent
of their wills, as one candle lighteth another, and of
the conjunction of their females (called *leannain sith*,
or fairy lemans, like the succubae mentioned of old)
with superterraneans and their Merlin-like monstrous
or giantly productions thereupon; and of the unfre-
quency of their visits and fearful appearances now, as
being out of their proper element (except they be sent
as a portent at some extraordinary occasion) since the
Holy Gospels flourishing among us; in respect of their
troublesome hauntings before-time, who (as strangers
and enemies invading other territories) left an affright-
edness of travelling in the dark in the minds of men
that dread mischief from them (yea, even persons having this second sight and seers themselves, though persons most conversant with them, find such horror and

trouble by the intercourse that they would often full gladly be as free from them as other men): these (to pursue at more length than I had now time for) I leave to the judgment and credit of everyone's particular inquiry and experience.

A SHORT TREATISE

OF THE SCOTTISH-IRISH CHARMS
AND SPELLS

1. It is not well known when and by whom this art of charming among the Scottish-Irish was first invented and broached, but sure the most of these spells relate to something in the Christian religion; some of them have words taken out of the Holy Bible, as Psalm 50.18, John 1.1, etc. Those that defend the lawfulness of charms call them a continued miracle, which by Heaven's compassion to men's infirmities convey virtue from all the hands they pass through, by reason of the sanctity of the first deviser, and to work in their kind, as a once-dedicated telesm in its own, both lasting in vigour for many ages, and they give that ancient instance in Psalm 58.4 of enchanting the adder from doing hurt for a precedent. Albeit assuredly charmers in Deuteronomy 18.11 be flatly discharged and reckoned up with necromancers, witches, and consulters with familiar spirits, and by experience it is found that such as come once in their reverence can never be rid of them, but will still have occasions that will need these white witches' assistance, in curing of one, when they kill another—and yet that the Holy Scriptures may borrow a comparison of obstinacy from the asp, as well as a caveat of wariness and wit from a thief in the night, and an unjust steward needed not be wondered at.

2. There be charms for all common diseases from top to toe, from the falling evil and convulsion of the sinews to the wen and excrescence on the eye-bree called *ceannaid*. Most of them are in way of prayer called *orrtha*, but said to be of more efficacy than any prayer now pronounced. The words notwithstanding are much corrupted in process of time by being transmitted through so many mouths, and 'tis not easy to reconcile them all to good sense or a meaning proper for the designed conveyance, besides that they are used by many of bad conversations and who do not understand much of what they utter: which makes others to suspect that the good words in the spells are but the policy of the counterfeit Angel of Light to train on the unwary to his lure, and that they being intended only as a watchword and sign of the compact with his followers, he is not scared to hear so many pious phrases (wanting the understanding and affection which is the life of all), specially since he was prompt enough to adduce Scripture-words to our Saviour himself in Matthew 4. As they are spoke by rote, so several of them were wont to be set down in rhythm. It was customary also with ancient practiced magicians for solemnity's sake, and to strike a greater reverence in the receivers of benefit by them, to change the names of ordinary things into those of creatures that had some like operation to that which they designed to bestow, so framing a sacred peculiar style of their own;

which yet did not alter the nature of anything they spoke of to any that could discern and distinguish, more than the Blessed Jesus (calling bread his body) changed the true nature of either (as some might instance now for their purpose). Then these words so consecrated were thought operative to all that gave credit to them and were their partisans, being once made partakers of their influence. Even the Platonists in their rites of lustrations and purifyings gave benefits, mystically signified under words of several representations, which words they thought were introduced by the gods, who knew the natures of things and were delivered by them to the first men that lived, who were called sons of the gods, and giants (in opposition to the *filii terrae*, idiots and weaklings), as immediately formed and then instructed by them. Hence the sacred language of their mysteries was believed to have a magical force from the gods to do the deed, which strong and vigorous force (but secretly conveyed) was restrained to these very words and points as delivered by tradition, without any voluntary alteration; and they reckoned their virtue evaporated and lost by being poured out and translated into any other language. The Jews also are very sly in translating any of the common forms of blessing or the like, prescribed in the law by mystical ways. Both the good spirit and image of Jesus's holy mind and life and also the malice of the Evil Spirit against all good are conveyed to men according to their different endeavours after them: it is not the natural influence that the pronunciation of such words can have on the things signified by them which brings the effect to pass, but purely the promise and authority of the first institutor on such persons and things as he has command over, and manifests it his pleasure so to bestow his power. Thus in a stable legal sense, every office hath its *vocabula artis* whose propriety is understood according to the occupation it treats about, whether sacred, civil, or profane; as what is cloth in the merchant's hand is called a cloak or coat when come through the hands of the tailor.

3. There be philtres used and other attractives of love by spells or words (as well as by other meretricious arts) that cause the person's beloved if but touched to follow the toucher, immediately losing all command of themselves, either by an unaccountable sympathy or some other invisible impulse—but how soon they lasciviously converse together, all that love dies into an envenomed spite. Yet the charmer dares give Elisha's following of Elijah when touched, and Simon and Andrew's relinquishing all to follow their true Master, for justifying of his pranks. In this receipt, besides the words, they bestow sometimes a dose composed of spittle and other liquidities called an *varigh ghraidh* (because having an addle egg (belike) intermixed). There is another charm called *sgiunach* that attracts the fishes

plentifully to the angler. But in the more usual charms of cure, besides a general prayer composed of some incoherent tautologies that is used before and after, called the *seachd phaidir*, or seventh and perfect prayer (set down hereafter), there are words instituted for transferring of the soul or sickness on other person's beasts, trees, waters, hills, or stones, according as the charmer is pleased to name, and the effect follows wonderfully, which scares many sober persons among the tramontanes from going in to see a sick person till they put a dog in before them or one that pertains to the house; for where charmers are cherished, they transfer the sickness on the first living creature that enters after the charm is pronounced, which creature readily rages with pain till it die. Thus this cheap way of healing distempers without physic does notwithstanding pay the account some other way, by sacrificing somewhat to the original healer, whoever be the instrument.

To pass these for the present with the briefs and amulets that make men proof against lead bullets, iron weapons, and the like, I will set down some of their more remarkable charms and spells as they are usually written and spoken, one in Latin, another in Irish, which I translate, and give the rest only interpreted for brevity's sake.

i. The general prayer, or Pater Noster, called *seachd phaidir*, repeated in way of preface and conclusion to every remarkable charm:

Mary is first placed, the Pater Noster of Mary, one, the P. N. or prayer of my King, two. Of Mary, three. Of the King, four. Of Mary, five. Of the King, six. The Seaven Seanings (or Salvations) to the Son of my King Omnipotent.

ii. The charm against the palsy and falling evil, written in paper and tied about the patient's neck:

In nomine patris et Filij et spiritus sancti, amen. Dirupisti Domine vincula mea, tibi sacrificabo Hostiam Laudis sed nomen Domini invocabo, nomen Jesus Nazarenus Rex Judeorum, Titulus Triumphalis, Defendas nos ab omnibus malis, Sancte Deus, Sancte Fortis, Sancte et immortalis, miserere nobis Heloj✝ Heloj atha✝ Messias✝ Eother✝ Immanuel✝ Pathone✝ Sabaoth✝ Tetragrammaton✝ on✝ eon✝ a thonay✝ alma✝ avala✝ Throne✝ Emanuel.

iii. The spell to expel the unbeast:

The order of Saint Benedict at the appointment of Inachus, to be set about the neck of the infirm, against the sharp-piercing beast, the unbeast, the white fistula, the brown cancer, the flesh cancer, the bone cancer—

Come out, thou piercing worm as my King appointed. Either die or flit thy lodging as Jesus Christ commanded. God and the King omnipotent either chase you out alive or slay you within.

These words the charmer speaks holding his two thumbs to his mouth still spitting on them, and then with both thumbs strokes the sore, which daily mends thereafter. They use spitting as an antidote against all that is poisonous and diabolical.

iv. A charm spoke in a napkin, and the napkin is sent many miles off to be tied about a child's open-head to lift it up (as they speak), and it does the fact.

I will lift up thy bones as Mary lift up her hands, as the forks are lifted under the Heavens, as the priest lifts up the upright mass, up to the crown of thy head. I lift the cheek-bones, the bones of thy hind-head, thy brow before and behind.

This they labour to justify as to its institution and operation by the report they hear of the weapon-salve and sympathetic powders, which they suppose may have some such words accompanying and aiding the natural and sympathetic application; which may derive virtue from a special favour of Heaven granted to the first inventor; or from the natural properties secretly conveyed; or from some odd invisible physician (as the actors command) that so swiftly carries away and applyeth the cure.

v. A spell, said to cure a swollen milt:

The skill against a swollen milt, to assuage its wrath, against the sharp milt, the rough milt, the bare milt, the brow milt, against the sharp-snouted grey worm that holes and eats the sinews of your heart and vitals.

But now the most dangerous point of this enchantment succeeds, which is the assigning a place for the evil, when expelled. (For the devils, say they, when put out of the man sought unto the swine.) Therefore thus the enchanter proceeds when he thinks meet.

He that gives warmth and prosperity, turn from thee all hill-envy (or fairy-envy), all son-malice, all man-malice, all woman-malice, my own malice with them. As the wind turns about the hillock, thy evil turn from thee (O Allex, or such), a third part on this man, a third part on that woman, a third on waters, a third on woods, a third on the brown harts of the forest, and a third on the grey stones.

There are spells also against bruises, swollen-cheeks called *goll ghalar*, the *tayyi*, or flux, toothache, being smitten with an infectious and evil eye (as they call it). There be knots with words, tied by a concubine on her paramour's hair, that will keep him from carnality with any other during her pleasure, an approved cure to it. The same knot is oft cast on a thread by sportful people when a party is a marrying, and before the minister, which ties up the man from all benevolence to his bride, till they be loosed, unless the charm be prevented to take effect by first saluting of the bride after the marriage is consummated and before they leave the churchyard and dedicated ground. But what is as strange as any, some charmers will extract a mote out of a person's eye at many miles distance, only they must first (spaniel-like) see and smell at something worn by the patient. The words which he mutters I have not attained, but his manner is to fill his mouth with water, laying his hands on it. When he has muttered the spell to himself, he pours the water out of his mouth into a very clean vessel and lets see that very mote in it, which molested the person's sight that he was informed of, who will be found free of it from the time of this action. Whether there be a secret reason that a charm has not so much efficacy when uttered by a woman as when by a man, or if because it was first devised by a man, continuing its vigour in the way it began, is not worth the while to dispute it.

These then are the exorcisms used for casting out of diseases and pains, as heretofore they were to cast out devils, whereof I have given a smattering to let see the many foolish conceits and dangerous customs in the critical and peremptory observance whereof many of the Scottish-Irish weary and burden themselves, to the great neglect of better usages and injunctions. They set about few actions all the year over without some charm or superstitious rite interwoven, which hath no visible natural connection with the affair about which 'tis made to further it. Yet herein they have been taught of old, to keep them in an implicit obedience, still busy and yet still ignorant, every age transmitting such supposed-profitable folly and reckoning it a greater *piaculum* to neglect such, than to transgress God's most holy and undoubted commandments.

This is the secret.

AN EXPOSITION
OF THE DIFFICULT WORDS IN THE
FOREGOING TREATISES

Abstruse	Hid, or shut up close.
Adapted	Being made very fit.
Addle	Rotten or spoiled.
Air	One of the four elements. The air which liveth, or is in the air.
Amphibious	He that liveth as well on water as on land.
Amulet	A preservative against enchantment, bewitching, or poisons, to be hanged about the neck.
Antidote	A counter-poison or a medicine against poison.
Antipodes	People which go directly against us, with the soles of their feet against ours.
Adscititious	Chosen, admitted, associate, or strange.
Astral body	An artificial body assumed by any spirit.

AN EXPOSITION OF DIFFICULT WORDS

Atoms	Motes in the sun, or a thing so small it cannot be divided.
Badgers	Broks.
Bier	A coffin that is reserved for the corpse of the poor people and kept within the church.
Boaz	In strength, meaning the powers thereof shall continue.
Candidates	They that stand and labour for any office clothed in white robes because among the Romans they used white robes; a suitor, or he that endeavoureth to obtain any thing.
Centre	The point in the midst of any round thing; the centre of a circle.
Chameleon	A little beast that doth easily change itself into all colours and is nourished only with the air.
Chimeras	A feigned beast.
Circumference	Compass.
Coalesce	To grow together or to increase.
Cockatrice	A serpent, killing man and beast with his breath and sight.

Cognizance	Examination, determination, or trial by a judge.
Colleague	A fellow companion or co-partner in office.
Colonies	Inhabitants sent to a foreign country.
Comment	Exposition.
Compact	Appointment or confederacy.
Condensed	Made thick or hard.
Convinctions	Assurances.
Deception	Beguiling.
Defaecat	Uncorrupt, pure, and clean from dregs.
Delphian	Two faced; ambiguous and doubtful.
Disquisition	Trial of a thing.
Drain	Dry up.
Echo	A sound rebounding to a noise or voice in a valley or wood; a resounding or giving again of the voice.
Element	The foundation of any thing, the first principal cause or instruction; whereof all things take their beginning, being four: fire, air, water, earth.

Elves	A tribe of the fairies that use not to exceed an ell in stature.
Entities	Beings.
Ether	The firmament, sky, light, brightness.
Exorcism	Conjuration.
Exuviae	A cast skin of a snake or adder.
Faculty	Virtue or strength in a thing, a power to do or speak.
Fanaticism	Fanatic = mad and foolish.
Fantastic	A foolish vain vision.
Fauns	A rank of daemons betwixt angels and man.
Gradation	A form of speaking when the sentence goes by degrees or steps going up in order one after another.
Helix	A kind of ivy, bearing no berries, running round.
heluo	He that in eating and drinking destroyeth his substance, as gluttons, wasters, and prodigals.
Heterogeneous	Of another kind.

Hypochondriac
Melancholy   A windy melancholy which is bred of ache and soreness about the short ribs, from whence a black phlegm arising doth hurt and trouble the mind.

Immersed   Plunged, drenched, or dipped in water.

Impetus   Violence, vehemency.

Insects   Any small vermin divided in the body, between the head and the belly, having no flesh, blood, or sinew, such as flies, gnats, pismires, or emmets.

Intellectual   Belonging to understanding.

Intrigues   Politics, secrets, or mysteries.

Jachin   He will establish his promise toward his house.

Legerdemain   Sleight of hand.

Legion   Is a brigade or regiment of 6,000 footmen and 732 horsemen.

Lychnobious   He that instead of the day useth the night and liveth as it were by candle light.

Magic   Witchcraft, sorcery, soothsaying.

Malefice	An ill, naughty deed, and mischievous act.
Meridian	Mid-day or noontide.
Mole	A moudewort.
Mole	A little brown spot in any part of man's body.
Necromancy	Divination by calling on spirits.
Noctambulo	He that riseth and walketh in the night time when asleep.
Nymphs	Goddess of waters; maids, or brides.
Obvious	Gentle and easy, or that which meeteth with one.
Optic	Pertaining to sight; *optici nervi*, the sinews that bring the virtue of seeing into the eye.
Oracle	A prophesy or prediction.
Orb	A world, a region, a country.
Parallel	Such-like.
Parelii	Two or three suns appearing through a refraction of a cloud.
Paroxysms	A rage, a fit of distraction, or rush.
Parson	A curate or parish priest.
Phantasms	Vain visions, false imagination.

AN EXPOSITION OF DIFFICULT WORDS

Phenomenon	An appearance either in the heaven or in the air.
Philtres	A love potion.
Plaginism	A stealing of menservants or children.
Propagated	To make, to spread, or to multiply.
Puppet	A baby, or image like a child.
Python	A prophesying spirit, or a man possessed with such a spirit, a belli-rummer, as it were the ill spirit speaking out of his belly.
Quaintly	Neatly, eloquently.
Rabbinical	Jewish.
Radicate	That hath taken root.
Receptacle	A place to receive and keep things safe in; a place of comfort or refuge.
Ricks	Stacks.
Rosicrucian	A possessor of a magical-like art.
Scrutiny	A diligent search.
Seer	Wizard, or a people of the second sight are they that telleth of things before or to come after.
Shrug	To be aversed.
Sirens	Sea monsters.

AN EXPOSITION OF DIFFICULT WORDS

Siths	People at rest and in peace.
Struma	King's Evil.
Suanoch	Mantle or cloak.
Subterraneans	Those people that lives in the cavities of the earth.
Succinct	Short or brief.
Superterraneans	Are we that live on the surface of the earth.
Tendons	Small things like hair hanging at the roots of trees, or a little vein.
Terrestrial body	Is a body made of the four elements.
Thesi	A position; the natural primitive word whereof other are derived and deduced, a termination.
Topical spirits	That haunt one place and not another.
Tragical	Cruel, outrageous.
Transmigration	A departing from one place to dwell in another.
Utopias	A nation invented by men's fancies.
Vehicles	Chariots, or a general name of all things serving to carry.

AN EXPOSITION OF DIFFICULT WORDS

Wight	A cunning man.
zijim jiim and ochin	Were either wild beasts or fowls, or ostrich or spirits, whereby Satan deluded man, as by the fairies, goblins, etc.

NOTES

5   *tramontanes.* Derived from the Italian and meaning literally "those who come from beyond the mountains," i.e., from beyond the Alps; by extension, and as used by Kirk here, northerners.

6   *defaecat.* Unsoiled, pure. See also Kirk's glossary.

6   *foison.* What can be harvested from something.

7   *champaign ground.* Open fields.

7   *sain.* To make the sign of the cross; to ward off evil by means of prayer or invocation.

8   *middle-earth men.* Humans.

9   *coacted.* Compelled, coerced.

9   heluo. A glutton. See also Kirk's glossary.

10 *Rachland.* Place unknown. Perhaps the Irish island of Rachlin.

11 *Gyges's ring.* Gyges (died c. 652 BC) was the king of ancient Lydia. In Plato's *Republic* Gyges is said to have been a shepherd who discovered a magic ring that, when worn, rendered him invisible, thus allowing him to kill his predecessor, King Candaules, undetected.

NOTES

12 *far-senting.* Able to perceive at a distance.

12 suanochs. Garments made from tartan, or sunach, material. See also Kirk's glossary.

13 *Endor Witch.* King Saul visits the Witch of Endor in order to summon up the spirit of the prophet Samuel (I Samuel 28.4–25).

15 *those men in Luke 13.26.* "Strive to enter in at the strait gate: for many, I say unto you, will seek to enter in, and shall not be able."

15 *mort-head.* Death's-head.

15 cuirp dhaondachbach. Meaning uncertain. *Cuirp* is Gaelic for "body."

15 totum. A whole.

15 *exuvious.* Cast off, shed, as a snake's skin. See Kirk's glossary entry "*Exuviae.*"

16 *Benjamites.* The Hebrew tribe of Benjamin was renowned for its skill at archery and slinging: "every one could sling stones at a *hair breadth*, and not miss" (Judges 20.16).

17 *fey.* Here doomed.

18 *peel.* To strip or pillage.

19 *illapse.* A coinage of Kirk's, from the Latin *illabor*, "to enter."

20 *plaginism.* Kidnapping. See also Kirk's glossary.

20 leannain sith. "Fairy lovers."

21 *as did Elijah (I Kings 18.42).* Elijah calls on God to send rain: "And Eli'jah went up to the top of Carmel; and he cast himself down upon the earth, and put his face between his knees."

22 *privado.* An initiate.

22 *Luke 1.20.* "And, behold, thou shalt be dumb, and not able to speak, until the day that these things shall be performed, because thou believest not my words, which shall be fulfilled in their season."

22 *Elisha ... (in 2 Kings 6.17).* "And Eli'sha prayed, and said, LORD, I pray thee, open his eyes, that he may see. And the LORD opened the eyes of the young man; and he saw."

22 *Peter (in Acts 5.9) foreseeing the death of Sapphira.* Sapphira and her husband, Ananias, were members of the early church who embezzled church funds. Peter denounced Ananias, and he fell dead. Sometime later Peter encountered Sapphira, who did not know what had happened to her husband. He denounced her as well, predicting that she would suffer her husband's fate—as she promptly did. "Then Peter said unto [Sapphira], How is it that ye have agreed together to tempt the Spirit of the Lord? behold, the feet of them which have buried thy husband are at the door, and shall carry thee out."

22 *2 Corinthians 12.4.* "He was caught up into paradise, and heard unspeakable words, which it is not lawful for a man to utter."

22 *2 Kings 5.26.* Elisha divines—"Went not mine heart with thee?"—that his servant Gehazi has taken payment for miracu-

lously curing a leper; he afflicts him with the disease as punishment.

23 *pythoness.* An oracle. Possibly referring to the angel who spoke through Balaam's ass. See Kirk's glossary at "Python."

23 *secret engines.* Snares or traps.

24 *prospectives.* A generic word for an object that enhances vision.

24 *adscititious.* Supplementary. See also Kirk's glossary.

24 *Mr. Greatrakes the Irish stroker.* Valentine Greatrakes (1628–1683) was a well-known healer who toured England curing the scrofula by the laying on of hands. He corresponded with Robert Boyle, who attested to the stroker's powers.

24 *the King's Evil.* Scrofula, or lymphadenitis, a disease of the lymph nodes that causes them to become greatly enlarged.

25 *Nazarites.* Group of Jewish ascetics—most famously Samson—whose vows include one that "there shall no razor come upon his head" (Numbers 6.5).

25 slinnenacd. From *slinnean*, Gaelic for "shoulder blade."

25 *trake.* A stroll or idle wander.

25 *the Marquis of Montrose, his wars with the states in Scotland.* James Graham, fifth Earl and first Marquess of Montrose (1612–1650). Montrose led several military campaigns on behalf of James I and James II in the 1640s.

26 in thesi. A stated claim.

26 *living image.* In some versions of the manuscript, "living" is rendered as "lingering."

27 *her name is NcIntyr.* It was not unusual, in the seventeenth and eighteenth centuries, for Scottish women to bear a female form of the traditional patronymic, following the pattern of the male patronymic, but substituting "n" for "m."

30 *English usurpers.* The Parliamentary government that had deposed and executed King Charles the First in 1649.

30 *ships and habits.* Clothing.

30 *species.* The outward appearance or visible form of something.

38 *mentioned by Aristotle in the fourth of his* Metaphysics*, if I remember right.* Not found in Aristotle.

39 *pragmatic.* Here meaning "active."

39 parelii. A parhelion, an illusory sun that under the right atmospheric conditions appears in close proximity to the sun itself. See also Kirk's glossary.

40 *cockatrice.* See Kirk's Glossary.

41 *salved.* Countered.

41 *Sadducees.* Denounced in the New Testament for their disbelief in the afterlife (Acts 23, passim).

41 *Socinians.* Followers of Faustus Socinus (1539–1604), Italian anti-Trinitarian theologian, resident for many years in Poland, who taught that Jesus, though uniquely free of sin, was not

himself divine. The Socinians are considered precursors of modern Unitarians.

43 *the learned lynx-eyed Mr. Baxter.* Richard Baxter (1615–1691), a nonconformist clergyman who wrote widely on theological matters and who was imprisoned for alleged libel against the Church of England.

44 *Dionysius Areopagitica.* Also known as Dionysius the Pseudo-Areopagite; an anonymous fifth-century philosopher whose mystical writings were for centuries wrongly attributed to an Athenian associate of Saint Paul.

44 *drolls.* Jesters.

44 *vehiculated species of spirits.* Embodied spirits.

44 *Cardano.* Girolamo Cardano (1501–1576), a prominent Italian physician, mathematician, and astrologer.

44 *Cornelius Agrippa.* Heinrich Cornelius Agrippa von Nettesheim (1486–1535) argued that all supernatural phenomenon were ultimately derived from God.

44 *the learned Dr. More.* Henry More (1614–1687), a philosopher and theologian affiliated with the Cambridge Platonists.

44 *noctambulos.* See Kirk's glossary.

45 *Deuteronomy 18.11.* "There shall not be found among you any one that maketh his son or his daughter to pass through the fire, or that useth divination, or an observer of times, or an enchanter, or a witch . . ."

46 *Raymond Sebond in his Third Book.* Raymond of Sabunde

(13??–1432), whose *Theologia Naturalis* argued for the unity of the natural and divine worlds, positing man as the connecting entity between the two. Montaigne translated the work (which was not divided into books) from Spanish into French.

47 *Mason Word.* A code word or other means by which one Freemason was held to recognize another. The phenomenon was often associated with Scottish Freemasonry and thought to have originated in Scotland.

47–48 *Jachin and Boaz, the two pillars erected in Solomon's Temple.* Freemasons claim the builders of King Solomon's Temple in Jerusalem as members of a proto-Masonic society. Masonic symbolism often incorporates or refers to this origin. See also Kirk's glossary.

48 *brieve.* A spell.

48 *dotages.* Fanciful stories.

49 *struma.* Another name for scrofula; see note at *King's Evil* at page 24.

49 αχμη. "Acme."

51 *Elisha, not intellectually only but sensibly, saw Gehazi.* See note at page 22.

51 sluagh saoghalta *and* sluagh sith. "Earthly people" and "fairy people."

52 *the* limbus patrum, *and* infantum. Respectively, the limbo of the fathers and the limbo of the children. The limbo of the fathers housed the souls of just men (e.g., Adam, Abraham, the prophets) who lived and died before the coming of Christ;

after the crucifixion and resurrection, they ascended with him to heaven. Unbaptized infants are said to be consigned to the limbo of the children, where, though not enjoying the eternal bliss of the saved, they are considerately spared the sufferings of the damned.

52 'εις αδμην. "Into Hell"

52 *third Heavens.* See 2 Corinthians 12.2: "I knew a man in Christ above fourteen years ago, (whether in the body, I cannot tell; or whether out of the body, I cannot tell: God knoweth;) such an one caught up to the third heaven."

54 *donations.* Offerings.

56 *intellectuals.* Mental powers.

57 *wramp.* Wrenching or twisting.

58 *furder.* Scots for "success."

59 Speculum Trinitatis...*which some call the beatific vision.* The ability of souls in heaven to observe God directly.

62 *lychnobious.* Nightwalkers.

62 *fairy lemans.* A leman is a beloved. The word is often used to describe a religious devotee, but here the connotation is more likely of an illicit lover.

62 *Merlin-like.* In some versions of the Arthurian legend, Merlin was reported to have a mortal mother and demonic father.

64 *telesm.* Talisman.

65 *the falling evil.* Epilepsy.

65 *eye-bree.* Can refer to the eyelid, the eyebrow, or the eyelash.

67 *Elisha's following of Elijah when touched, and Simon and Andrew's relinquishing all to follow their true Master.* Kings 19.20: "Elisha ran after Elijah, and said, Let me, I pray thee, kiss my father and my mother, and then I will follow thee." Matthew 4–20: "And Jesus, walking by the sea of Galilee, saw two brethren, Simon called Peter, and Andrew his brother, casting a net into the sea: for they were fishers. And he saith unto them, Follow me, and I will make you fishers of men. And they straightway left their nets, and followed him."

67 varigh ghraidh. "Love posset."

69 In nomine patris et Filij et spiritus sancti, amen...The spell is a mishmash of mangled Latin, Greek, Hebrew, and Aramaic, including phrases from the Missal, the Psalms, and Jesus's cry on the cross: "My God, My God, Why hast thou forsaken me?"

70 *milt.* Spleen.

71 *consummated.* Here meaning solemnized or consecrated.

72 piaculum. A sin.

76 *an ell in stature.* Measurement of six hands' breadths, conventionally about forty-five inches.

77 *pismires, or emmets.* Ants.

FURTHER READING

David Baird Smith, "Mr Robert Kirk's Note-book," *The Scottish Historical Review*, vol. 18, No. 72 (July 1921), pp. 237–248.

Jo Bath and John Newton, "Sensible Proof of Spirits: Ghost Belief during the Later Seventeenth Century," *Folklore* 117 (April 2006), pp. 1–14.

Angela Bourke, *The Burning of Bridget Cleary: A True Story* (London: Pimlico, 1999).

Nicola Bown, *Fairies in Nineteenth-Century Art and Literature* (Cambridge University Press, 2001).

Hubert Butler, "The Eggman and the Fairies," in *The Sub-Prefect should have held his Tongue, and other essays,* R. F. Foster, ed. (Penguin Press, 1990), pp. 102–112.

John Gregorson Campbell, *Witchcraft and Second Sight in the Highlands and Islands of Scotland* (Glasgow: J. MacLehose and Sons, 1902).

Stuart Clark, *Thinking with Demons: The Idea of Witchcraft in Early Modern Europe* (Oxford University Press, 1997).

Judith Devlin, *The Superstitious Mind: French Peasants and the Supernatural in the Nineteenth Century* (Yale Univerisity Press, 1987).

FURTHER READING

Maureen Duffy, *The Erotic World of Faery* (London: Cardinal, 1989).

W. Y. Evans-Wentz, *The Fairy Faith in Celtic Countries*, Kathleen Raine, ed. (Gerrards Cross: Colin Smythe, 1977).

R. F. Foster, *W. B. Yeats: A Life, vol. 1: The Apprentice Mage, 1865–1914* (Oxford University Press, 1997) and *vol 2: The Arch-Poet, 1915–1949* (Oxford University Press, 2003).

Carlo Ginzburg, *Ecstasies: Deciphering the Witches' Sabbath*, Robert Rosenthal, trans. (University of Chicago Press, 2004).

Michael Hunter, introduction to *The Occult Laboratory: Magic, Science and Second Sight in Late 17th-Century Scotland* (Bury St. Edmunds: The Boydell Press, 2001).

Samuel Johnson and James Boswell, *A Journey To the Western Islands of Scotland with The journal of a tour to the Hebrides* (Knopf, 2002).

Robert Kirk, *The Secret Commonwealth & A Short Treatise of Charms and Spells,* Stewart Sanderson, ed. (London: The Folklore Society, 1976).

Hugh Miller, *Scenes and Legends of the North of Scotland* (Arno Press, 1977).

Karl Miller, *Electric Shepherd: A Likeness of James Hogg* (Faber and Faber, 2003).

Diane Purkiss, *At the Bottom of the Garden: A Dark History of Fairies, Hobgoblins, and other Troublesome Things* (New York University Press, 2000).

94

A. Ross, *The Folklore of the Scottish Highlands* (London: Batsford, 1976).

Carole G. Silver, *Strange and Secret Peoples: Fairies and Victorian Consciousness* (Oxford University Press, 1999).

Keith Thomas, *Religion and the Decline of Magic Studies in Popular Beliefs in Sixteenth- and Seventeenth-Century England* (London: Cardinal, 1997).

OTHER NEW YORK REVIEW CLASSICS

For a complete list of titles, visit www.nyrb.com or write to:
Catalog Requests, NYRB, 435 Hudson Street, New York, NY 10014

Also available as an electronic book.

ANDREY PLATONOV Happy Moscow
ANDREY PLATONOV Soul and Other Stories
J.F. POWERS The Stories of J.F. Powers*
CHRISTOPHER PRIEST Inverted World*
BOLESŁAW PRUS The Doll*
ALEXANDER PUSHKIN The Captain's Daughter*
QIU MIAOJIN Last Words from Montmartre*
QIU MIAOJIN Notes of a Crocodile*
RAYMOND QUENEAU We Always Treat Women Too Well
RAYMOND QUENEAU Witch Grass
RAYMOND RADIGUET Count d'Orgel's Ball
PAUL RADIN Primitive Man as Philosopher*
FRIEDRICH RECK Diary of a Man in Despair*
JULES RENARD Nature Stories*
JEAN RENOIR Renoir, My Father
GREGOR VON REZZORI The Snows of Yesteryear: Portraits for an Autobiography*
TIM ROBINSON Stones of Aran: Labyrinth
TIM ROBINSON Stones of Aran: Pilgrimage
MILTON ROKEACH The Three Christs of Ypsilanti*
FR. ROLFE Hadrian the Seventh
GILLIAN ROSE Love's Work
LINDA ROSENKRANTZ Talk*
LILLIAN ROSS Picture*
WILLIAM ROUGHEAD Classic Crimes
CONSTANCE ROURKE American Humor: A Study of the National Character
SAKI The Unrest-Cure and Other Stories; illustrated by Edward Gorey
JOAN SALES Uncertain Glory*
TAYEB SALIH Season of Migration to the North
JEAN-PAUL SARTRE We Have Only This Life to Live: Selected Essays. 1939–1975
ARTHUR SCHNITZLER Late Fame*
GERSHOM SCHOLEM Walter Benjamin: The Story of a Friendship*
DANIEL PAUL SCHREBER Memoirs of My Nervous Illness
JAMES SCHUYLER Alfred and Guinevere
SIMONE SCHWARZ-BART The Bridge of Beyond*
LEONARDO SCIASCIA The Wine-Dark Sea
VICTOR SEGALEN René Leys*
ANNA SEGHERS The Seventh Cross*
ANNA SEGHERS Transit*
GILBERT SELDES The Stammering Century*
VICTOR SERGE Memoirs of a Revolutionary
VICTOR SERGE Notebooks, 1936–1947*
VARLAM SHALAMOV Kolyma Stories*
SHCHEDRIN The Golovlyov Family
ROBERT SHECKLEY The Store of the Worlds: The Stories of Robert Sheckley*
CHARLES SIMIC Dime-Store Alchemy: The Art of Joseph Cornell
WILLIAM SLOANE The Rim of Morning: Two Tales of Cosmic Horror*
SASHA SOKOLOV A School for Fools*
VLADIMIR SOROKIN Ice Trilogy*
VLADIMIR SOROKIN The Queue
NATSUME SŌSEKI The Gate*
JEAN STAFFORD The Mountain Lion
RICHARD STERN Other Men's Daughters